One Night Stand

A Martin Family Novel

Parker Kincade

Editor
Lacey Thacker

Cover Artist
Pickyme

Formatted by
JTLW Design

This book contains content that is not suitable for readers who are 17 and under.

ISBN: 978-1-5061116-4-3

DEDICATION

For D.R. Your faith in me never wavered and you never complained when I locked myself in a room to write. I love you.

And for Joe. Your persistence and subtle wit kept me on my toes, but it was your heart that kept me going. You will always be my first.

PROLOGUE

"Honestly Amanda, he wasn't good enough for you," Samantha said as she tossed back a shot of cinnamon whiskey.

"You never complained about him before."

"What was I supposed to say? 'Hey, I think your boyfriend is a douche'? Yeah, right." Sam snorted. "That would have gone over well."

Another shot.

"That's exactly what you should have said," Amanda huffed, but she knew Sam was right. Dammit. "Are you here for moral support or to get drunk?"

"The two have to be mutually exclusive?"

Amanda snickered at her best friend.

"I'm the one who got cheated on, and you're the one getting drunk. How does that work again?"

"Wasn't planning on doing it alone." Sam winked as she sailed a tiny tumbler across the table to her.

Amanda poured the fiery liquid into the glass and took her

shot. She shuddered, embracing the warmth that infused her body and mind, and she relaxed for the first time in days.

"So"—Sam waved a finger at her—"do the three horsemen of the apocalypse know about it yet?"

Her brothers. Sweet Jesus, when they found out it was going to get ugly. And potentially bloody. Those boys did love a good fight. She almost felt sorry for Scott. Almost.

"God, no. I have enough to deal with without adding those three to the mix. They seem to think their sole purpose in life is to defend my honor." She rolled her eyes. "What they end up doing is just irritating the crap out of me with their Neanderthal bullshit. I don't need to be bailing their asses out of jail, again I might add, because they've got testosterone poisoning."

Amanda considered her friend. "You know they hate it when you call them that."

"All the more reason, my friend. All the more reason." The gleam in Sam's eye was sinfully wicked as she raised her shot in silent toast.

"What the hell is wrong with me?" Amanda blurted, hating the pitiful twang of her voice. "I'm getting a serious complex here. I mean, what am I supposed to do now?"

She stared into her empty shot glass like she'd find the answer magically spelled out at the bottom.

"Call the horsemen. Set up the ass kicking. Sell tickets." Sam giggled like a five-year-old.

Amanda narrowed her eyes, letting a sound of pure frustration pass her lips.

"Fine." Sam slammed her empty glass on the table so hard it shook. "Want to know what I think? I think you need to get laid."

Amanda's head fell back on the edge of her chair. "That's your answer for everything."

"Maybe not the answer to everything, but it sure would help

you get your mojo back." Sam's tone became serious. "Listen, Amanda, you need to get away. Take a vacation. Find a gorgeous stranger and have wild monkey sex with him. Be spontaneous." Sam smiled at her as she refilled their glasses.

Amanda tossed back her shot. "I fail to see how that's going to help me."

Sam gave her a droll stare. "Of course you fail to see how it will help. That's precisely why you need to do it."

CHAPTER 1

Amanda Martin pulled her car into the parking lot. She stared at the small building that served as the local watering hole before she turned off the ignition and slumped back in her seat.

Cheated on again. This must be some kind of record.

So far, the only two serious relationships she'd had were colossal failures. It took her first ex all of six months to jump into another bed. Well, that she knew of anyway. Chances were he'd cheated long before coming clean, telling her he just couldn't see himself with her forever. As if she were deficient or something.

She'd convinced herself that Scott, her most recent of disasters, was different. He was charismatic and sweet. Okay, so the sex wasn't mind-blowing, but they'd had it on a regular basis. So what the hell happened?

She'd caught the bastard in bed with another woman.

His secretary. *Jesus.*

She snorted in disgust. She didn't know if she was madder

that he'd cheated on her or that he'd turned her into a cliché. She figured she should be way more pissed off about the cheating. The fact that she wasn't meant she'd wasted the last year of her life on average sex with a guy she didn't really care about. Wouldn't that make her family proud?

And now here she sat in all her pathetic-ness, feeling sorry for herself.

In the parking lot of a bar in Nowhere, Texas.

What the hell am I doing?

Amanda liked the stability of a steady relationship. The idea of bouncing from man to man just didn't appeal to her. But maybe Sam was right. Maybe it was time for her to change her ways. Shake things up. Maybe a one-night stand was just what she needed. After all, she was young and relatively attractive.

She could do this, couldn't she?

Right. Time to buck up or shut up.

The gravel crunched under her boots as she made her way across the parking lot. Two cars flanked the front door and she breathed a sigh of relief that the place wouldn't be overly crowded. She tried to act casual, stopping just inside the door to let her eyes adjust to the light—or lack thereof.

The smell of stale beer and peanuts hung heavy in the darkened interior. Tables were spread around the perimeter of a small, open area she assumed was used for dancing. The jukebox belted out an old Hank Williams tune while its neon glow permeated the light haze of cigarette smoke. The other side sported a shuffleboard table and a pool table, along with several stray chairs turned this way and that. The bar ran the length of the back, with doors on each end, one marked *Private* and the other indicating restrooms beyond. She sauntered toward the bar, the butterflies in her stomach the only betrayal of her nervousness.

Two men played pool, swaying and obviously drunk, and

eyed her curiously as she slid onto a barstool. They both wore jeans that had seen better days, worn through the knees and streaked with dirt. Their grease-stained T-shirts and ball caps made her wonder if they'd rolled out from underneath a truck before walking in here.

The taller of the two offered her a calculating smile, showing off the yellow stain of his teeth.

Maybe this wasn't such a good idea.

"What'll ya have, miss?" The bartender asked, keeping a purposeful eye on the two playing pool.

"Whiskey. Straight up." She'd gone for confident, but ended up just sounding cheesy. All she needed was to fist bump the bar and she'd be in an old Western.

"Whiskey. Right," the bartender said with humor in his voice. "You're not from around here, are you?"

Thank you, Captain Obvious.

"No, I'm just here for the week. I've got a place not far from here."

"I see," he said, raising his brows in surprise. "So, what brings you to our fine establishment?"

He slid a drink to her.

"Fine, huh?" Amanda looked around. "Guess I was lucky to find a seat," she joked.

He flashed her a gorgeous smile. Stretching his arms out, he indicated to the rest of the room. "You just missed the rush. Ten minutes ago we were packed to the gills."

The mischievous gleam in his eye told her he was lying. He was working for what would probably be the only tip he saw all night. Amanda laughed, swirling the amber liquid around in her glass before taking a sip.

"Name's Jacob, but most folks just call me Jake."

"Nice to meet you, Jake."

He considered her a moment. "You got a name?"

She laughed again, blushing. She really needed to work on her flirting skills. "Amanda. My name is Amanda."

"Nice to meet you, Amanda." His gaze darted to the two men slowly approaching the bar.

"Yeah, Amanda," the taller of the two said, "it's very nice to meet ya." He took the bar stool to her left while his buddy chuckled and stumbled to the seat on her right. They stunk of alcohol and cigarettes, the combination making her eyes water.

Oh, this was a very bad idea.

"No trouble in here tonight, boys," Jake warned. "Back off."

"Aw, we don't want no trouble, Jake. We just wanna talk to the li'l lady here." The man to her left reached out to touch her hair.

"Let's *not* with the touching, big man." Amanda veered away. There were some things she wouldn't stand for. Invasion of her personal space was definitely one of them.

"That's enough, Clete." Jake crossed his arms over his chest. "Not gonna say it again."

Amanda slammed back the rest of her whiskey, ignoring the fact that it fried a hole in her stomach as she signaled Jake for another. "Hey, Clete"—she looked him dead in the eye—"how about I buy you and your buddy a beer and you go back to your game of pool?"

Then I can get the hell out of here.

"You're a mite more in'eresting than playin' pool, sweet thang." Clete weaved toward her.

Amanda boldly pushed at the man's chest. "While that may be so, I'm much more interested in being left alone."

"She's got a mouth on her, that's for sure." Clete's buddy leaned in until she could feel his breath on her neck.

Amanda's blood began to boil. She didn't need this shit. She was here to blow off some steam, not be harassed by a couple of smart-assed drunks.

"Get. Off." Amanda shoved her elbow into the man behind her. Having grown up with three brothers, she had no doubt she could defend herself, but she had enough common sense to know when it was time to go. Sliding off her bar stool, she reached into her pocket for cash to pay for her drink. She noticed Jake moving toward her side of the bar.

"Where you goin', li'l lady?"

She felt a hand slide over her ass. Amanda froze.

Oh, hell no.

Before she could stop herself, she balled up her fist and swung around hard. She made contact with the man's jaw with a sickening *crack*.

"Listen up, fuckwit," Amanda spat as she watched Clete fall from his bar stool and land on the floor with a thud. A mixture of adrenaline and fear caused her voice to quiver. "I told you not to touch me."

She flexed her hand. Yep. That was gonna hurt in the morning.

Jake was there in a heartbeat, placing himself between her and the men. Better late than never, she supposed. His palms were up to each side, his dark eyes darting between them as if he wasn't sure who he needed to protect from whom.

Clete was still on the floor, his buddy laughing over him. "She sure showed you, Clete," his friend slurred.

"Shut up, Ernie." Clete glared at Amanda, retribution burning in his eyes.

That's it.

She'd thought she would come here to unwind with a drink or two. Maybe find a gorgeous guy to have sex with. Now she was pissed, her hand hurt like the devil, and all she wanted was her couch and an ice pack. And maybe to kick Sam's ass for talking her into this little fiasco in the first place. And maybe another bottle of whiskey.

She wondered if Jake would sell her a bottle for the road.

A voice, low and full of menace, drifted from behind her just seconds before she felt him. Well, not so much felt as sensed. Like a rabbit would sense it was about to become coyote kibble. His heat penetrated her back. Amanda stiffened as she felt his hands move over the skin of her arms, hovering but not actually touching.

"What the fuck, Jake?" he growled.

Amanda spun to look at the man behind her and came face-to-face with his pecs.

Oh. Wow.

Her gaze roamed upward. He was well over six feet tall. Over six feet of powerful male. His black T-shirt strained against the pressure of containing all those muscles. Before she could stop herself, she leaned forward to take in his scent. Her head spun as the dizzying combination of leather and sandalwood drifted through her. She turned away before he noticed the heat that flooded her cheeks.

"It's under control, Joe," Jake snapped.

Joe pointed at the two drunkards. "You have one minute to get your shit and get out of my bar." He gently, cautiously, touched her arm. "Are you okay, slugger?" His mouth was so close to her ear she could feel his breath on her neck. His husky voice reverberated down her spine. The heady combination caused a reflexive shiver to run through her body.

His eyes narrowed dangerously on Clete. Clearly mistaking her reaction for fear, he growled, "Make that thirty seconds." He eased protectively in front of her.

Clete swore an oath as he pushed to his feet and stumbled toward the door. His friend followed close behind. Joe led her back to the stool she'd just vacated. "Here ... sit." His large hands engulfed her shoulders as he bent to look into her eyes. "Slugger?"

Amanda got her first good look at him. Her mind went blank. A strong jaw that narrowed slightly at the tip of his chin sported a dark five o'clock shadow. His lips were red and full and entirely too inviting. Jet-black hair fell in disarray around his face, thick locks waving across his forehead. And he had the bluest eyes she'd ever seen. Eyes that were narrowed in concern for her.

She cleared her throat. "Amanda," she rasped. Okay, so she *could* talk. Sort of. "I'm Amanda."

"Amanda."

Good Lord!

Her name on his lips was like a caress that went all the way to her core. She went instantly wet. She clenched her legs together and took a deep breath.

"You okay, Amanda?" he prodded.

"Yes, I'm fine." *Aroused.* "Just pissed off." She shot a glare at Jake. "And where the hell were you?"

Jake's jaw clenched. "What do you mean—"

"Shut the hell up, Jake. What you need to do is thank your lucky stars you're my brother or I'd be kicking your ass all over this county, get me?"

Amanda couldn't hold in her surprise. "Wait. You"—she took advantage of the opportunity to peruse his delicious male body from head to booted toe—"are related to him?" She nodded toward Jake.

"Look Amanda, I'm sorry," Jake said. "No excuses. I should have thrown them out the minute they approached you. I don't know what got into them tonight. Normally they're harmless."

Her anger immediately deflated. "It's not your fault, Jake. I should have just walked away." She sighed. "I know better." She looked back to Joe. God, he took her breath away. Jake was cute, sure, in that boyish I-wanna-make-out-with-you-in-the-back-of-a-Chevy way. But this man, with his long legs encased in tight, faded jeans that seemed to bulge in all the appropriate places, was a work of art. Carved by the gods to bring women to their knees. And speaking of knees, the package he was sporting certainly made her want to get on hers.

Focus, Amanda.

He gave her a half smile and extended his hand. "I'm Joe. Owner of this bar and"—he waved his hand at his brother—"the better looking of the two."

Jake snorted something that sounded a lot like "You wish," as he brought around a towel full of ice for her hand.

She reached to return the greeting, remembering too late the punch she'd thrown. Joe seemed well aware of her discomfort, gently cupping her hand in both of his.

"Vicious right hook you got there, Mandy."

"I have brothers," she said. As though that explained everything. At some point she'd regain her brain function. As soon as he stopped looking at her. And touching her.

Oh God, please don't stop touching me.

"Brothers who taught their sister how to fight?" His eyes danced with amusement.

"Overbearing, overprotective, and over-in-my-face brothers who wanted to make sure I'd never be taken advantage of." She smiled sweetly. "I'm sorry. I didn't mean to cause trouble."

Joe drew back in surprise. "I'm not entirely sure what happened before I came in, but I'm fairly certain it wasn't your fault." He reached out and tucked her hair behind her ear. "Wanna tell me what happened?" He took the ice pack from Jake and placed it delicately across the back of her hand.

She hissed as the rough towel scraped her sensitive knuckles. "It's no big deal. Couple of drunks getting handsy. It wasn't anyone's fault. It happened so fast. I overreacted."

"I'm sure you didn't overreact." Joe's voice turned hard again. "Those two are a pain in my ass." He shared a knowing look with Jake. "And they've just had their last beer here."

"They were almost a pain in my ass, too," she joked. "But I'm good. Won't be the first time I've nursed sore knuckles."

"You fight a lot then, slugger?"

She laughed at that. "Did I mention that I've got *three* brothers?"

He gave her a smile that had her nipples aching and pushing through her T-shirt. She squirmed in her seat, which only served to rub the seam of her jeans harder against her pulsating clit. She bit back a moan. *So this is what it feels like to be aroused to near pain.* She was close to throwing herself at him, audience be damned. Anything to relieve the tension building in her panties.

Joe noticed her distress. She watched as he slowly took stock of her. She knew the minute he saw the pearled buds of her chest, protruding shamelessly for his inspection. His jaw clenched and his back stiffened. She dared a quick glance at his lap. She hoped his back wasn't the only thing that had turned rigid. His eyes narrowed; his nostrils flared as if he could smell her arousal.

She watched in fascination as his gaze turned dark, smoky.

What would it be like to spend the night in the arms of a man like him? What kind of lover would he be? The thought caused her insides to turn to jelly. There was only one way to find out.

"Are you sure you're okay, Mandy?" His voice was hoarse. His fingers were stroking her palm as he continued to hold her injured hand. She desperately wanted him to be stroking her somewhere else.

It's now or never.

"That depends." Amanda gave him a seductive smile. "You wanna get out of here?"

Joe shook his head, his expression filled with genuine confusion.

"Excuse me?"

Amanda felt her face grow hot with embarrassment. This man was a walking god and here she was, Miss Plain-and-Ordinary, propositioning him. What was she thinking?

She stood a little too quickly, causing her bar stool to wobble before righting itself again. "Never mind. Sorry." She threw two twenty-dollar bills on the bar. "This should cover it." She hollered thanks to Jake as she made her way to the door.

"Mandy, wait."

Chapter 2

"Where is she?" Caleb Martin slammed the door and glared across the desk at Samantha.

"Jesus, Caleb." Her hand flew to her heart as she leaned back in her chair. "Knock much? You scared the hell out of me." She took a deep breath. "We really need to work on your people skills."

Caleb placed his knuckles on the desk and slowly leaned in. "Where. Is. She?"

Sam took her time smoothing her dark auburn hair away from her face. "I can see this is going to be a one-track conversation, so let me make this easy for you. Get out."

He walked around to her side of the desk and perched himself on the corner. He crossed his arms over his chest and settled in.

"Nope."

Sam glared at him as she hit the Intercom button on her phone. "Caroline? Call Security."

She heard her assistant chuckle. "Ah, sure thing, Miss Quinn."

"I *am* your security," the annoying male on her desk replied dryly.

"Good, that'll save us some time. Escort yourself out." She waved her hand to shoo him off.

"I'm not going anywhere until you tell me where my sister is."

Sam narrowed her eyes at the man sitting on her desk. Tall, blond, and commanding, with eyes the color of emeralds when he was pissed. And yep, two shining emeralds were fixated on her.

He'd never made any bones about the fact that he didn't like her. For years they'd argued and fought, needled and picked.

Now he barges in here without so much as a word, clearly showing how little respect he has for me.

God, she didn't think there was a man on the planet that drove her crazier than this one, so she felt perfectly justified in giving a little of that crazy back to him.

And she knew just what buttons to push.

Tossing her hair off her shoulder, she revealed her cleavage. "Nope."

Caleb's gaze cast to the skin she revealed. "I'm not leaving."

Pig. "Suit yourself, but you may be more comfortable in a chair." She gave him an irritated stare. "There are plenty in the conference room down the hall."

She could see the muscles in his jaw working overtime as he reined in his temper.

"She's been missing for three days."

Samantha rolled her eyes. "Not missing, you dolt. Away. There is a difference."

"Away, where?"

"Nice try, horseman. But my lips are sealed. She's in a

'no-man' zone." She hesitated a moment and laughed wickedly. "Well, a 'no-brother' zone, anyway."

"What does that even mean?" Caleb made a noise that sounded suspiciously like a growl. "What did you do?"

"Me? Why on earth would you think I did anything?" She blinked innocently.

Amusement flashed in his eyes a second before he got in her face. "Need I remind you of the time you got Amanda arrested for attempting to bribe an officer?"

"Charges wouldn't stick. We were framed."

"How about the citation for indecent exposure?"

"Case of mistaken identity."

"The bar fight?"

Her shoulders slumped a little. "Okay, that was—"

Caleb threw his hands in the air as he surged to his feet. "For the love of God, you're a lawyer!"

"Damn good thing for us that I am, too."

"Tell me where she is."

"No."

"Samantha."

She lowered her voice to mimic him. "Caleb."

"Jesus." He shoved his hands through his thick, blond locks. "You're the most annoying—"

"Be careful how you finish that sentence, horseman. Remember, I have what you want." She wagged her eyebrows suggestively.

"Stop calling me that," he snapped. "Contrary to popular belief, I'm not the harbinger of chaos."

Sam barked out a laugh.

"*That* is debatable. But I'm still not telling you where she is." She sighed at the stern look he threw her. "In case you've forgotten, Amanda is a grown woman. Perfectly capable of making her own decisions without your approval or, hey, even your input." She returned to the papers on her desk, dismissing him. "Time to cut the cord, big guy."

"Why didn't she tell us where she was going?"

Sam rolled her eyes again. "Seriously? One guess." She threw her hand up to stop him from answering. "No, wait, I'll go ahead and tell you because you're sure to get it wrong. She needs time alone. She needs space."

"Space? Space from what?"

She screamed in frustration. "You're unbelievable! Just leave her be, Caleb. She's fine. She isn't in any danger, and she'll be back before you know it. Stop being the controlling older brother for one second and let her do her thing."

She reached up to rub her temples. Yet again, her dealings with Caleb Martin caused her head to throb. Today was definitely one of those days she regretted relocating her private law practice into the offices of Martin Tactical and Security. She cursed Amanda for talking her into it after her old office had been broken into and vandalized. What good was cheap rent, secure or not, when she had to work from home? Pressing the Intercom button again, she said, "Caroline, please forward my calls to my cell. I'm working from home this afternoon."

"Where do you think you're going?" Caleb barked.

"You deaf?" She slammed a file closed. "Home. To work. Since it's obvious I won't get anything done here today." She stuffed a handful of files into her briefcase and slung it over her shoulder.

"Dammit, Samantha, I'm done playing with you." Caleb looked dangerously close to losing his temper. He pressed forward until they were nose to nose. "I want to know where my sister is, and I want to know right now."

Not cowed in the least, Sam smiled at him. "If she wanted you to know where she was, she would have told you. You think I'd betray her trust?" She blinked teasingly.

Caleb sneered. "I think you'd betray your own grandmother if it suited your purpose."

Ouch.

Sam felt the sting as if he'd slapped her. "Fuck you, Caleb," she said as she shoved past him, "and the *horse* you rode in on."

* * *

I'm such an ass.

Caleb watched Samantha stalk away. He hadn't meant what he'd said. Hell, he didn't mean most of what he said when he talked to her, but he wouldn't apologize for it either. That woman pushed his buttons something fierce, and she knew it. So, no. He wouldn't apologize. Not to Samantha. His sister had taken off to parts unknown, and he wanted to know why. If it had anything to do with that idiot she'd been dating, well, then he and the boys were about to have a little fun. He was responsible for her. For all of them. He wouldn't let them down again.

Their parents had been killed twelve years ago, leaving a deployed Caleb in charge of his three grieving siblings. Amanda had been the worst. He'd returned home to find her livid at him for being away, unwilling to even give him the time of day. Not one word.

For a whole year.

He'd struggled to regain her trust, and he wasn't about to let her pull away again. Period. He was the head of this family and if there was something going on, he should know about it. And he definitely knew there was something going on. Just as he knew Samantha was at the heart of it. Another one of her harebrained ideas, no doubt.

He, Brandon, and Alec had all been calling Amanda's cell for the last three days. Oh, she'd called back all right. She left a voice mail on the receptionist's phone over the weekend when she knew no one would be there to answer. Said some shit about getting away and that she'd be okay. Caleb knew he was overreacting, but he somehow couldn't stop himself. *Good God, I'm a controlling bastard, aren't I?*

"Well played, brother." Caleb glanced up to see Alec, the younger of his two brothers, leaning in the doorway.

"Shut up." Caleb pushed past him into the hallway. He ignored a scowling Caroline as he walked by and continued down the hallway to the elevators that would take him to his own office. Alec fell into step beside him.

"You knew we were tracking her. Why did you even bother going to Sam?" Alec asked.

"Thought it would be faster." Caleb hit the elevator button.

"Right. Faster." Alec spit out a laugh. "How'd that work out?"

"Swimmingly."

Alec snorted. "You two have been dancing around each other for years. When are you gonna admit you've got a thing for her?"

Caleb punched the button for the elevator again. "You're out of your fucking mind if you believe the bullshit you're spewing. That woman is a menace. I haven't known a moment's peace since she and Amanda became friends. Don't think I don't remember who's responsible for that." Caleb glared at a guilty Alec.

"Hey now." Alec raised his hands in defense. "I like Sam. She's been good for
Amanda and you know it."

Caleb pinched the bridge of his nose, biting off his retort. Whether he liked it or not, Samantha had been the only one to get through to Amanda after their parents died. Which was the whole reason he tolerated her in the first place.

"You realize Amanda will have our balls on a platter when she finds out we tracked her." Alec leaned against the wall next to him. "I, for one, like my balls right where they are."

"As long as she's safe, I couldn't give a rat's ass how mad she gets."

Another punch of the button. Where the hell was the elevator?

"Wait, *tracked* her? As in no longer tracking? You know where she went?"

Alec drew out a sigh. "Of course we found her. She's not hiding."

Caleb responded with a hard fist to Alec's shoulder. A devilish smile crossed Caleb's face as the elevator doors opened. This day was looking up. He slapped Alec on the back, pushing him into the elevator.

"Let's grab Brandon and go see what our little darling is up to."

CHAPTER 3

Joe couldn't believe his ears. Did Amanda just ask him if he wanted to leave with her? Before he could recover his shock, she was hightailing it out the door. From the moment he'd walked into the bar tonight, he'd been captivated. First by the way she defended herself, next by the vulnerability he felt as he'd held her hand, and then by the way she looked at him as if he were a treat she'd like to eat.

Now he was just plain curious. He'd had women come on to him before. What surprised him was his desire to follow through with this one.

"Hold up, sweetheart." He snatched her money off the bar. "Jake's gonna cover your tab tonight, aren't ya, Jake?" Joe looked at his brother expectantly.

Jake shrugged. "Sure, no problem."

"Give me one minute." Joe walked behind the bar and grabbed a full bottle of whiskey. "Don't leave," he added as he caught her looking between him and the door.

Jake wagged his eyebrows. "Someone's finally gonna get laid," he taunted.

Joe smacked him on the back of the head as he walked by. "Just for that, dickhead, you can pay for this bottle too." He tried to sound irritated, but he just couldn't keep the smile from his voice.

It had been a long time since a woman had caught his interest and it felt nice. He'd spent his life avoiding commitments. His former job with the military wasn't really conducive to the white picket fence kind of lifestyle. He'd been alone most of his life, refusing to get attached to anyone or anything. But this woman...

Damn, she looked good. She dug her hands deep into the pockets of her low-riding jeans as she tapped the sexiest pair of cowgirl boots he'd ever seen against the concrete floor. Her blonde curls tumbled downward, teasing the lower part of her back where her T-shirt had ridden up. Imagining the feel of all that temptingly tanned skin under his tongue made his mouth water. He swore he could already taste her. He grunted as his cock swelled at the thought of licking every inch of her.

He was suddenly very glad he'd stopped in tonight.

Joe held the bottle up as he approached her. "Whiskey okay?"

Her vibrant green eyes latched on to his. "Sure."

Smiling, he just barely resisted the urge to lean in and kiss her. Instead he trailed his fingers across the exposed skin on her back, resting his palm in the sexy little bend above her belt. The feel of her warm skin had his already engorged erection pressing painfully against his zipper.

"Ready?"

"Sure," she said again.

"Things are gonna go very well for us tonight, Mandy, if you stay so agreeable," he teased with a wink. He chuckled at her sharp intake of breath as he guided her out the door.

The cool air hit them as they walked outside. Amanda was quiet beside him as he led her across the gravel to the only car left in the parking lot that didn't belong to Jake. Joe had ridden in on his Harley and there was no way he was putting her on the back of his bike without the proper gear.

He glanced at her apologetically. "While I'd love to take you for a ride on my bike, tonight isn't that night. Only one helmet," he said at her puzzled frown. "I can follow you or…" He waited to see if she'd jump in, hoped she'd jump in. Anything to get her talking. "Mandy?"

She shook her head slightly. "No, no. It's chilly out. Why don't you ride with me?"

"You okay to drive?" He looked at her with mock sternness and gently raised her abused knuckles to his lips. That earned him a sweet smile.

"I'm sure I can manage."

Joe sighed and let her hand drop. Maybe she was having second thoughts. He wasn't sure what had caused her to close off all of a sudden, but one thing was for sure—he was going to play this out. He suddenly wanted to break down her walls and see what was there. He wanted to hear her laugh. He wanted her to cry out his name in pleasure.

He wanted her naked.

Oh yeah, he was going to play this out. "Lead the way, Mandy. I'm all yours."

* * *

What the hell am I doing?

She'd just picked up a strange man in a bar and was taking him back to her secluded ranch house.

They make really scary movies about this kind of stuff.

Amanda glanced at the man riding shotgun. She felt a

twinge of guilt that she planned to use his body and walk away in the morning, but holy crap! Had this guy hit the mother lode or what? His tall, sinewy frame ate up the space of her compact car.

I'm all yours.

His words drifted through her mind and she bit back a moan.

"Mandy?"

Her gaze shifted back to the road. "You know, you're the only one who's ever called me that."

"You don't like it?"

"I didn't used to," she muttered. She had the feeling she wouldn't care what this man called her, as long as he was naked and whispering in her ear.

Joe gave her a knowing look and chuckled. "Mandy it is then." He settled back for the ride. "I like that there's something of you that's solely mine."

"Really?" Amanda couldn't imagine why he'd want that. Or why the thought of it made her heart race.

"Yeah." He seemed surprised by his own admission. When he looked at her, there was a playful twinkle in his eye. "So, where are we headed?"

"I have a place not far from here."

"You live here?"

"No." She hesitated. "I live outside of Austin."

"Just on vacation then?"

She shrugged.

He appeared to consider her carefully before he asked, "Are you married?"

"God no!" she said in a burst of laughter. Then she sobered. "Are you?" She hadn't thought about that. Her white-knuckled grip on the steering wheel caused little sparks to ignite in her palms. *Please say no.* No way she was sleeping with a married man.

Or any man involved with another woman.

"Not married."

Whew. "Attached?"

"Attached?" He laughed harshly. "Nope. Not attached."

"Oh, well, that's good then." She turned off the road onto a wide lane. A sign stood in a proud arch above them as she drove through.

"Fawn Glade?"

Her smile was one of genuine pleasure. "My dad used to call this our 'retreat ranch.' We used to spend long weekends and holidays here." As they continued down the drive, the large log home she'd always loved came into view. "He bought the property and had the house built when I was just a baby."

The house was large and had an inviting porch that surrounded it on all sides. She'd been happy to find that caretakers had done an excellent job in keeping the house clean and ready. Amanda had had to stock the refrigerator, but the pantry shelves were full, the linens fresh.

She gestured toward the corral as she pulled to a stop. "Back then we each had our own horse. I learned to ride out here. My brother sold all of them a few years after our parents died. He said it wasn't fair to keep them out here when we hardly visited anymore." A wave of sadness went through her as she looked at the empty area. It seemed an injustice to let the space go to waste.

She jumped as his hand brushed along her thigh, surprising her out of her thoughts.

"Easy, there. I lost you somewhere."

She was suddenly so nervous she thought she might throw up. "Sorry, I, um, I was just thinking."

"Second thoughts about inviting me over?" His fingers brushed across her cheek as he gently cupped her face.

"No, it's just … I know better than to bring a strange man

to my house where we will be alone and away from civilization, and now you know where I live and—"

He held up his hand to quiet her rant. "Everything out here is away from civilization," he drawled. "If it makes you feel any better, I've never been to this house, but I know the area. I was born here. I live here full-time now. I know the sheriff personally." He ran his hand through his hair. "Jesus, Mandy, I'm going to fuck you, not murder you."

Her eyes widened in shock at his bluntness. Moisture flooded her panties as she thought about what he'd do to her. "I have to be honest with you." She hesitated a moment before continuing. "I don't have the first clue what I'm doing. My last two relationships were alike in that the only thing they were concerned about was their own pleasure. Both ended with them in bed with other women."

Amanda's voice rose somewhat and the words tumbled out. "I'm here because my idiot best friend suggested I get laid. The kind of laid where I can take my pleasure and walk away. 'Find a gorgeous stranger and have wild monkey sex with him,' she said." Amanda blushed as she gave him her best Samantha impression, not that he'd know the difference. "I've never had sex like that before."

She choked out a whisper. "What if I'm no good at it? What if that's why men keep running around on me?" Amanda was horrified that she seemed to have no control of her mouth. "And now you're here, and I don't have the first clue what to do with you." She couldn't breathe. "I'm not very experienced, and you're the most amazing-looking—"

"Amanda, stop." Joe put two fingers over her lips. "I get that you're nervous. Honestly, I'm a little nervous myself. It's not every day a gorgeous woman waltzes into my bar and asks me to go home with her."

He had to be kidding. "I'm sorry. Look, I'll take you back to the bar. You probably have better—"

He grabbed the back of her neck and crushed his mouth to hers. He didn't wait for permission, just thrust his tongue against her lips and demanded entrance. She opened slightly, and he dived in. She moaned as his tongue grazed over the edge of her teeth, darting back and forth until he gently sucked her tongue in to play. The heat of his mouth was like warm brandy and honey, causing her body to burn with need. His muscles bunched as she moved her hand along his thigh. She wanted to feel every inch of him.

The contact seemed to break the spell. He tore his mouth away from her, resting his forehead against hers. In the quiet car, the sound of their dual panting was as erotic as the kiss itself.

He cleared his throat. "Maybe we should go inside?"

"Inside. Right. Yes." Her hands were shaking as she reached for the keys.

"Here," he said easily. "I got it." He grabbed the keys and the bottle of whiskey and unfolded himself from her car. She got out and met him as he walked around. His arm went around her waist as he lifted her off the ground.

Joe brought his mouth back to hers, nibbling on her bottom lip. She opened immediately and sucked his tongue into her mouth.

He took hold of her ass and lifted her off the ground. "Wrap your legs around me, Mandy."

Her arms locked around his neck and she eased her legs around him. Another moan escaped as his hard cock pushed against the seam of her jeans. Her pussy tightened as heat consumed her.

The silky strands of his hair tickled her cheek as she lowered her mouth to his ear. She delighted in the shiver that went through him as she circled the inner curves with her tongue. Feeling bold, she laved him from collarbone to earlobe, causing him to stumble.

"Jesus, Mandy. You're killing me." He swatted her ass. "Behave for a second." He set her on her feet at the front door and waited for her to let them inside.

She fumbled before pushing open the door and leading him through the house to the kitchen. Grabbing the whiskey he still held—how the hell he'd managed to keep that in his hands she'd never know—she went to the cabinet for shot glasses. "I think I need a drink," she mumbled. "You?"

"We don't have to do this," he said, even as he reached out to cup her neck.

She smiled, barely keeping the wonder from her voice as she brushed her fingertips across his jawline. "You really mean that, don't you?"

"Yes," he said without hesitation.

She glanced pointedly at the erection straining against his jeans.

He gave her a sly smile. "I never said I didn't want to. But no means no, Amanda. About that, I make no concession. If you want to stop, it stops. Now."

Joe dropped his hands and stepped back from her.

She moved back into him. He was so warm. She savored the feel of his hard frame pressing against her. "What if I just want to make out for a while?" she teased, her gaze glued to his lips. "You have the most amazing mouth."

Did I just say that out loud? Sam would be so proud.

He made a throaty sound as he leaned in and brushed his lips over hers. His touch was light, playful, utterly intoxicating. He traced the line of her jaw with his lips.

"Making out with you does have intense possibilities." He lifted her chin, forcing her to look at him. "Is that what you want?"

"Is that enough for you?"

His lips quirked. "I don't relish the thought of going home with a hard-on, but I meant what I said. You control what happens here tonight, Mandy. You understand?"

The dominance that bled from his voice made her stomach clench. She gave him a quick nod. "Right. No teasing." Which suited her just fine. She was on fire and ready to give him whatever he wanted.

He laughed, a deep, masculine sound. "Oh no, Mandy," he assured her, "there will be teasing, and hopefully, a whole lot more."

She hissed in a breath as he nipped her shoulder.

"You okay with that?"

She moved her hips, caressing him with her pelvis. Yes, yes, she was very much on board with that idea. And she was done talking. Her clit pulsated. She wanted him.

Unable to wait another second, she grabbed the hem of her T-shirt and yanked it over her head. His breath hitched as he stared at her. She was glad she'd chosen to wear the bra and panty set that Sam had gifted her with just for this occasion. The bra was an incredibly sexy, see-through lace that did nothing to hide her darkened nipples. Nothing like the basic cotton bra she wore every day.

"My God, you're beautiful," Joe whispered, a second before he grasped the material and twisted. The clasp broke under his hand, the thin lace falling away to reveal her rose-tipped breasts.

"Hey," Amanda protested even as her womb convulsed, "that was new!"

He ignored her as he rolled his tongue over a taut peak. "Your nipples are so pretty, Mandy. So hard, so ready for me to taste." The heat of his mouth seared her as he sucked her nipple into his mouth. His teeth tugged gently before he released her and blew lightly across the tip. She arched her back as he pressed her into the counter. Desire overtook her as he latched onto her other breast. Every flick of his tongue against her tightened bud raised her need higher and higher. No one had ever made her feel this way before. She was desperate for relief.

"Joe, please," she begged as he feasted on her breast.

"Bedroom," he demanded. "I'm not taking you the first time on the kitchen counter." He smiled wickedly. "But it does have possibilities for the third or fourth time." He licked her nipple again before pulling her upright.

"I don't care about that. Here is good. Now is better." She reached for his shirt and began pulling it up.

He bent and scooped her into his arms. "Unless you want me to wander aimlessly around this house, you'll point me to your bedroom."

"Top of the stairs on the left."

He took the steps two at a time. He was barely breathing hard as he carried her into the bedroom and set her on her feet. "Get on the bed."

"You're awfully bossy," she said, moving to obey him.

He gave her a wink. "You've got no idea." He stripped off his shirt, revealing a glorious amount of hard, tanned skin. Her mouth watered. She needed to see the rest of him.

She crawled to her knees as he approached, and reached out to caress the hard expanse of his chest. She ran her tongue around the dark edge of his nipple, delighting when it drew in tight. His stomach rippled as she traced the lines of his abs, each muscle prominently displayed for her feminine pleasure.

She frowned, noticing a scar that ran along his stomach and disappeared around his side. Sliding from the bed, she followed it around behind him, trailing her fingertips across his shoulder blades, down his back, and lower into the waistband of his jeans. He groaned loudly as she cupped the hard globes of his ass in her hands and squeezed. She slipped her arms around him, freeing the button of his jeans. "I want to taste you," she said, facing him again.

"Mandy," he warned as she fell to her knees.

She slowly peeled his jeans open, releasing the heavy length of his erection. Of course a guy as sexy as Joe would go commando. She licked her lips hungrily. His legs twitched when she reached for him. She wrapped her fingers delicately around his length, coming up short of meeting in the middle. He was larger than any man she'd been with before. Excitement boiled her blood as she opened her mouth and took him in.

* * *

Joe didn't think he'd ever seen anything as erotic as Amanda's mouth wrapped around his cock. He forced his hips to be still while she struggled to find her rhythm. Her mouth was stretched wide as she took him to the back of her throat.

"Tilt your head back, sweetheart," he encouraged. "Relax your throat. Yeah, Mandy, that's it. Just like that."

His head fell back as he teased the back of her throat once again. She clamped a hand down on him as he tried to move, holding him firmly in place. She swallowed, sending a bolt of pleasure through his dick and up his spine.

"Sweet Jesus." He was about to lose his ever-loving mind.

She released him with a soft *pop*. Her tongue darted out to capture the bead of moisture that seeped from the head before moving down to caress the seam between his balls. He drove his hands into her hair and pulled her mouth back to where he wanted it.

Her smile was pure sin the moment before her heat enveloped him. The sight of her lips, swollen and wet, was driving him mad. And she was still wearing those damn cowgirl boots.

Her cheeks hollowed as she sucked him in. He held her head in place as he pumped into her mouth. Her moan sent a tantalizing vibration through his balls, and he fought the need to come.

The sight of her reaching back to rub herself through her jeans was too much. More than he could take. He grabbed the base of his cock and squeezed. Hard. No way he was blowing the first time in her mouth. His body jerked in protest as he pulled away from her. "Enough."

She blushed and looked at the floor. "Did I do something wrong?"

"Are you kidding me?" He pulled her to her feet. "Look at me, Amanda."

As her eyes met his, something inside him broke. His tough little slugger was gone. There was no denying what was shining in her eyes now.

Doubt. Fear. Insecurity.

He kissed her lips, swollen and sexy as hell from being wrapped around him. "You were great, baby." He trailed his lips down her neck, kicking the rest of the way out of his jeans. "You'll have another opportunity to finish me off, I promise you." He traced lazy circles up her spine as his lips met the curve of her collarbone. He inhaled her scent, an intoxicating combination of vanilla and jasmine. "I want to be inside you."

"So what are you waiting for?" She kicked out of her boots. Her chest rose and fell in rapid succession as she unbuttoned her jeans. She eased them off, revealing the long length of her tanned legs.

He chuckled deep in his throat. "Some things shouldn't be rushed." His fingertips brushed across the swell of her breasts. "This is most definitely one of those things."

Amanda gasped as he pinched her nipples and gave them a light, delicious twist.

"Ah, you like that."

Her face flushed with the heat of arousal. "Y-yes."

"What else do you like?" He nudged her ear, his breath warming the space between them.

She stared at him. "I-I don't know."

Joe pulled away slightly and raised a brow at her. "You don't know? You've done this before, haven't you?" He gave her an amused smile.

"Of course I have," she huffed.

"But you don't know what you like?" God, this woman intrigued him. So full of passion one minute, so unsure of herself the next.

Her skin flushed. She shrugged and gave him a tentative smile.

"Hmm, this is quite a quandary, Mandy." His tongue danced out, drawing sinfully down her neck. "So, you don't know if you like it soft and easy"—he rolled his hips and pressed a kiss to her shoulder—"or if you like the rough stuff." He bit her shoulder lightly at the same time his hand returned its torment on her nipple. Her sweet cry was his reward. "Or maybe a little of both," he mused. "Tell me, Mandy, have you ever had anyone in your ass?" Her skin felt like satin. He trailed his fingers down to caress the line of her panties.

Her belly fluttered under his teasing fingers. "No, never. It … it's not something I want to try."

He eased her onto the bed, hovering over her. "Is that so? Adventurous girl like you?"

"I've heard it's painful." She wrapped her legs around him and tried to pull him down on top of her.

"It's the ultimate show of trust and respect." He dipped his head down to taste the sweet nectar of her lips. "You have to trust your partner to protect you. To show you the immense pleasure that's found when you let yourself go."

Her eyes were dazed with lust. "I wouldn't count on that." She whimpered as his hand brushed against the wet seam of her panties.

He chuckled. "There are so many things I want to do to you right now, Mandy. But first, I'm going to taste you." He traced the line of her lips with his tongue. The smoky flavor of whiskey mixed with a hint of molasses went straight to his head. "Your mouth tastes so good. I wonder ... does your pussy taste as sweet?" He didn't give her time to answer. "I bet it does." He pressed his mouth to her ear. "I'm going to fuck you with my tongue and fingers until you're crazy with need." He grabbed the edges of her panties and moved with them as he worked them down her legs. "Then I'm going to bury my cock deep in your sweet pussy until you scream my name."

"I'll scream your name now," she breathed, "if it will get you started."

She trembled as he stared at the lips of her pussy, glistening and free of feminine curls. He ran his finger through her wet slit. "You shave."

"W-wax. Samantha's idea." She jerked as his fingers circled her opening.

"So smooth ... so soft." He spread her moisture over the satiny lips. "God, Mandy. I want to go slow," he began, "but damn." He attacked her with his mouth. No preliminaries, no hesitation.

"Oh God!"

He slid his tongue over her sex, groaning as her wetness coated him. "So good." He pulled back long enough to ease a finger inside her. Heat clamped down and surrounded him. He added a second finger. "You're so tight, Mandy. I can't wait to be inside you, baby."

"Joe, please," she begged. Her head thrashed as the in, out, in, out of his fingers drove her higher and higher.

Her cries were driving him crazy. "That's it, baby, come for me." He worked his fingers and clamped his mouth over her clit.

* * *

Amanda had never felt anything as good as Joe's mouth on her. His fingers stroking deep in her pussy set her skin on fire. Tension coiled deep in her belly. She was close. So close. She just needed…

"Come for me, Mandy," Joe demanded. He took her tender nub in his mouth and sucked hard.

She clawed at the comforter as a million tiny sparks exploded through her body. She arched, pressing her hips against his mouth, and screamed his name. Wave after wave of sensation convulsed through her. The walls of her vagina gripped him as evidence of her pleasure coated his sinful fingers. Her head spun as she fought for solid ground.

She was vaguely aware when he moved from her. "You're so beautiful," he whispered, kissing a trail up her still quivering belly. Another wave of pleasure hit her as he slid his fingers into his mouth. "Like honey," he murmured as he licked the digits clean.

"I've never felt anything like that," she panted.

"We aren't done yet." He settled himself between her legs. "Now we're going to see if you can take all of me, Mandy. You're so tight, baby, do you think you can?"

No one had ever talked to her like this during sex. Usually it was just groan, groan, oh God, annnnnnnd done. His words excited her, made her want to play along. He made her feel sexy.

She gazed up at him, her eyes still lazy with desire. "Mmm, you're pretty big, but I think I'm up for the challenge." She reached between them to grip his length. They both hissed as she trailed the head through her wet slit.

"Shit, Mandy wait," he snarled, "condom. I don't have a condom." He pushed himself away from her with a vicious curse.

"Basket on the side table. Hurry." She smoothed her hands down her body and ran a finger through her own wetness. "You don't want to miss what's next."

Joe's eyes flared. "Do that again."

Planting her feet on the bed, she tilted her pelvis up and inserted her finger deep. She watched his eyes flame as she brought the wet finger to her lips, mimicking his earlier action. She slowly sucked it into her mouth, tasting her own juices. She was tempting him and she knew it, gloried in it.

So this is what Sam meant about getting my mojo back.

Joe didn't take his eyes off her as he reached for the basket. "What's this?" He reached in and cursed. A burst of lust crossed his face as he looked at her again. "Mandy?"

"Present from Sam." Her face grew warm as he looked through the contents of the basket.

"Vibrator, lube … Christ almighty." He turned his face to the ceiling. "A vibrating butt plug… Remind me to thank her," he said as he found the box of condoms and tore it open. "Remind me to thank her a lot."

His gaze turned predatory as he pulled out a foil-covered package and tossed the box on the bed. "Does the thought of using those toys excite you?"

She licked her lips as he sheathed himself.

"Does the thought of using those toys with *me* excite you?"

Yes, yes, yes! "Maybe."

He laughed and crawled up her body until they were nose to nose. "Let me taste those sweet juices." His tongue pressed lightly against the seam of her lips. Her hips cradled him, and she shamelessly rubbed herself against his straining erection. He was hot and hard against her.

"I can't wait." She reached between them and fisted his cock. She held him against her entrance and pushed up with her hips. Dual moans filled the room as he filled her a scant inch.

He *was* big. She winced as he stretched her. The burning that surrounded her opening caused every nerve ending in her body to sing.

She tightened her legs around him as he eased out. "No!"

His voice was strained. "I'm not going anywhere, baby, don't worry." He eased forward again. "Ah, God. Need to go slow. Don't want to hurt you. So tight." The words were forced through clenched teeth.

She could feel the restraint he was using to go slow. His muscles were shaking with it. But she didn't want slow.

"I want you to fuck me, Joe. Now." She secured his ass with her ankles and surged up with her hips.

* * *

Joe yelled out as she forced him deep. Her heat surrounded him as he fought for control. One wrong move and this was going to be over before it got started. "Are you okay?" He looked down to see her wearing a satisfied smile. Her inner muscles squeezed him and the telltale sizzle of his own release began at the base of his spine. "Jesus. Be still."

"Don't stop." Her hands dug into the skin of his ass as she tried to pull him closer.

"Dammit, Mandy." He surged his hips hard and buried himself to the hilt. "Hold on to me."

She grabbed his shoulders and he began to fuck her with a vengeance. Each powerful flex of his muscles drove him deep into her moist heat, her cries of pleasure urging him on. "Can't. Mandy. Too good." Each word was driven home by the powerful force of his thrusts. His breath came in harsh bursts. He reached between them and rubbed his thumb against her clit, giving her what she needed to take her over the edge.

She screamed as she bucked beneath him and he felt her release just an instant before he found his own. His eyes rolled back in his head as her pussy stroked and milked him dry.

"Fuck." His cock jerked inside her, causing yet another ripple of pleasure to shoot through his balls. He collapsed on top of her, loving the feel of her soft skin underneath him.

Amanda sighed as she wrapped her arms around him. Her voice drifted through his afterglow. "So that's what all the fuss is about."

"What?" His head snapped up, his mind instantly racing. "You weren't a virgin," he asserted. He was still buried balls deep in her heat. He would've known if she had been. Besides, she told him she'd done this before, hadn't she?

"Of course I'm not." She sighed again. "It's just … well … it was my first orgasm, or actually the second if you count when you used your mouth." She paused before going on. "I mean, with a man."

"With a … wait … what?" Damn, she was adorable when she blushed like that. Something she did a lot, he realized.

"I mean"—she traced her fingers over her nipples—"I've made myself—"

He groaned. "Stop." He placed his hand over her mouth. "Just stop talking." The image of her pleasuring herself filled his cock with blood. He'd just had the hardest orgasm of his life and his cock was already ready for round two. His cock might be ready, but he wasn't. She'd be sore if he didn't give her time to recoup a little. They had all night and he intended to take advantage of it.

Amanda gasped as she felt him growing hard inside her. "Really?"

He eased from her and bent to place a kiss on her nose. "Not yet. Let's take a break, maybe rest a little." His voice turned ominous. "I'm not even close to being done with you."

Her laughter rang in his ears as he rolled from the bed and headed to the bathroom. He disposed of the condom and returned to the bed with a warm, wet rag for her. Her eyes stayed closed as he cleaned her. Throwing the rag aside, he stretched out next to her, tucking her close to his side. As if she couldn't stop touching him, she ran her hands over his chest and down his abs. He grabbed her wrists when she started for his groin.

"Oh no you don't. Rest first, play later."

She stuck her tongue out at him playfully but allowed him to pull her back against his chest.

"How did you get this scar?" she asked as her fingers returned to wandering across his skin. She was going to be the death of him for sure.

"Knife," he replied.

She raised her eyes to his. "That's it? What kind of answer is that?" She continued to caress him.

"An honest one." He shook his head when he realized she wouldn't let it go. "It happened a long time ago, Mandy. It's not worth talking about." His body tingled under her wicked fingers and he again grabbed her wrist. "As much as I love your hands on me, if you don't stop, I'm going to end up fucking you again." He pressed a kiss to her forehead. "And you need to rest because I promise you, we aren't done."

She closed her eyes and relaxed. "That scar looks like whoever had the knife meant to gut you." She snuggled deeper into his arms. "I'm very glad they weren't successful."

He chuckled as he felt her go limp. "Me too, Mandy. Me too."

He gazed at her as she slipped off to sleep. She was beautiful; there was no doubt about that. Her curls were soft against the pillow, her lips swollen and pouty from his kisses, her cheeks still flushed. He stroked his hand over her slender waist, coming to rest on the flare of her hip. He hadn't shared anyone's bed for a long time, but never in his life had he experienced the pleasure this woman had given him. He loved the feel of her hands on his body. He loved the way she'd come undone in his arms. He loved the way she'd lost herself in him, turning doubt and insecurity into bold temptation.

He'd followed her because she intrigued him. Now he wasn't sure one night would be enough. Now he wasn't sure he could ever get enough. He pulled her closer and closed his eyes as he contemplated the deep need that settled in his chest.

He didn't know how long he'd been out when he came to the awareness that they weren't alone in the house. He frowned at the clock. He hadn't slept long at all.

As if she also sensed danger, Amanda came awake with a start. Joe tightened his grip around her to keep her in place. "Mmm." She snuggled deeper into his hold, pressing her ass into his groin.

"Shh, stay still," he murmured into her ear. He kept his arms locked around her.

"What time is it?"

"It's just after midnight," he whispered.

"Why are you whispering?" she whispered teasingly back at him.

She froze as the sound drifted through the room. Heavy booted footsteps on the hardwoods below. From the sound of it, several sets of booted feet.

"Son of a bitch," she hissed under her breath.

"Amanda!" Her name boomed through the entire house.

She groaned and tried to sit up, but Joe held fast.

"Let. Me. Up." Amanda pried his fingers apart and wiggled out from underneath him. She grabbed a robe and quickly wrapped it around her naked body. "Don't worry, I'll be right back." She held her hand up to hold him off. "Stay put."

He watched her race out the door.

Did she just order me to stay put?

He had no idea who was bellowing her name throughout the

house. No mistaking it, the bellower was male … and sounded angry.

Stay put, my ass.

He jumped up, pulled on his jeans, and went after her.

Chapter 4

"Jesus, Caleb, do you have to be so loud?" Amanda complained, strolling into the kitchen to see not one, but all three of her brothers.

Caleb leaned against the sink, his boots crossed at the ankle, arms crossed at his chest. His massive form seemed to take up the whole kitchen, and damn if he didn't look unhappy. Very unhappy if the scowl on his face was any indication.

"What's up, little sis?" She glanced at Alec, who was just three years older than her, as he sat at the table and helped himself to a fistful of her peanut M&M's. He offered her a playful smile as he popped one in his mouth. "We didn't wake you, did we?"

Brandon didn't say anything, but rose from his seat across from Alec with a warm smile and wrapped his arms around her.

She'd admit, alone they were impressive. Together, they were downright intimidating. They'd all inherited their father's light hair, chiseled jaw, and rough edges. They might look like golden boys, but looks could be deceiving. Each was over six feet of solid muscle and bad attitude.

And she loved them more than anything in the world.

"Actually, yes, you did." She returned the hug. Suddenly remembering she was naked under her robe, she pushed him away. "What are you doing here?" She wiggled to adjust the robe tighter around herself. "And by you," she motioned to each of them, "I mean all three of you."

"What do you mean taking off like that?" Caleb's voice was deadly calm and right to the point.

Amanda let out a dramatic sigh. "I'm twenty-seven years old, Cay. Jeez, get a grip."

"I don't give a good goddamn how old you are. You can't just take off without telling anyone where you're going. And by anyone," he sneered, "I mean the three of us."

"You didn't seem to have any trouble finding me," she snapped back. "What the hell is your deal anyway?"

"Everything okay, slugger?"

Shit shit shit.

Amanda spun to Joe as he walked into the kitchen. He immediately stole her breath. His hair was sleep-tousled and hung just slightly over his forehead. The button of his jeans was undone, and they rode low on his hips. His bare chest rippled as he reached out and tucked a piece of hair behind her ear. Images from earlier bombarded her. His cock in her mouth, his head between her thighs, his tongue buried deep inside her. She bit back a groan as she felt her nipples harden. She could feel the warmth of her skin heating to a bright red.

Great. Blushing. Hard nipples. Naked under her robe with the interrogation brigade standing behind her. Perfect.

"Slugger?" Brandon.

"Did he just call you slugger?" Alec.

"Jesus Christ, Sterling. What the fuck are *you* doing here?"

"Caleb!" She whirled on him.

"Don't start with me, Amanda," Caleb said. "I'm not in the mood."

"Like I give a shit about your mood when you bust into my house bellowing like I'm one of your trainees or something."

"*Our* house, kitten. Not *yours*," he pointed out, using the pet name he'd given her as a child. "And why the hell did this man just call you slugger?" He jabbed his finger toward Joe.

Joe leaned in. "Um, Mandy, is there something I should know here?" His gaze never left Caleb. "You said you weren't married."

She heard snickering coming from the table as she turned back to Joe.

"God, no." She placed a hand on his chest and let his warmth seep into her. "My brothers," she whispered, rolling her eyes so only he could see. "This house belonged to our parents."

"Ah, good news then." He gave her a sexy smile. He nodded at Alec and Brandon, blatantly ignoring Caleb. "Joe Sterling. Friend of Mandy's."

Caleb narrowed his eyes on him. "*Mandy's?* I'll repeat, what the fuck are you doing here, Sterling?"

Joe gave him a tight smile, but Amanda could feel the aggression coming off them in waves.

Amanda turned a glare on Caleb. "Will you be civil?" she hissed. "Wait." She glanced at Joe and back at Caleb. "You two know each other?"

Caleb ignored her question. "You mind telling us what you think you're doing here, *Mandy*? Without a word to your family that you were taking off? Wait, don't answer that." He perused her from head to toe. "It's obvious what you've been doing here."

This time, she let them see her eyes roll. She knew from experience that there'd be no reasoning with Caleb when he was this riled up. Continuing the argument would be absolutely pointless and probably just piss him off worse. Which was exactly why she kept going.

"Fuck off, Caleb. Jesus, I'm a grown woman. How many women have you had in your bed this week? Or you?" She turned to Alec, who raised his hands in mock surrender. "Or you?" She looked pointedly at Brandon, who was studying the wood grain in the table. She crossed her arms over her chest. "Don't you think you're overreacting just a little?"

"Overreacting?" Caleb laughed. "That's rich coming from you. Your boyfriend dumps you and not a week later you're fucking some stranger you just met." His hand came down on the counter with a loud crack. "When, Amanda? Last night?"

She cringed.

Joe snaked a protective arm around her waist, offering his silent support.

"That's enough, Caleb," Brandon warned. Alec leaned back in his chair, casually popping M&M's into his mouth while he glared daggers at Joe.

Caleb towered over Brandon in a heartbeat. "Don't you fucking tell me when it's enough, Bran. She can't just run off when things get hard, scaring us half to death in the process. It's irresponsible and," he turned back to look Amanda in the eye, "childish."

"We all want answers, Cay," Brandon said gently. "But you know as well as I do browbeating her isn't going to get us anywhere."

"And neither is talking about me like I'm not in the room. Get over yourself, Caleb. I'm not shutting you out or running away from you. You're just pissed because you didn't get a say. I made a decision without you, big deal. Can't a girl take a fucking vacation if she wants to? If anyone here is acting *childish*, it's you." She ran her hands through her hair in frustration. "And he didn't just dump me, as you so graciously put it."

She swallowed back tears. She really didn't need this shit right now. "Just how the hell do you two know each other?" She felt Joe's arm flex around her waist as she changed the subject.

Alec was apparently done sitting on the sidelines. "Did he hurt you?" Pop went another M&M. Although he appeared casual, she noticed his hands were clenched into tight fists.

"Who, Joe? No, of course not!"

"Not Joe," Alec murmured.

Instantly the room went deadly still.

God, this is a nightmare.

It was bad enough to be humiliated by the cheating bastard who was supposed to care about her. Now she had to share her humiliation not only with her brothers but also with the man who'd just given her the best sex of her life.

She couldn't keep the defeat from her voice. "No, Alec. It wasn't like that." A collective breath from the males in the room eased the tension a bit.

"Well then, why don't you fill in the blanks for us. 'Cause all we know is we've been calling you for days and you didn't feel the need to answer any of our messages. Did you not, for one minute, believe we'd be worried about you?" Caleb apparently had two volumes tonight: loud and louder.

"I left you a message." She took a deep, cleansing breath. "Jesus, I have my own shit to deal with. I'm sorry if calling you back wasn't high on my list of priorities. You knew I was okay, whether you want to admit it or not. There's just some stuff I've got to work out on my own. And I'd really appreciate it if you'd stop yelling at me, Cay."

Caleb snorted. "What I should really do is paddle your ass."

"I could take care of that for you," Joe offered politely, drawing everyone's attention.

Amanda elbowed him in the ribs. "You're so not helping right now."

Caleb's eyes flashed. "Just what've you been doing with our little sister?"

Amanda balked as Joe maneuvered her behind him, smiling a lazy smile. "You really want me to answer that?"

Caleb growled and lunged as Alec and Brandon jumped up from the table. Joe ducked, grabbing and twisting Caleb's arm behind his back. Once his hold was secure, he pushed Caleb's face into the cabinets a little harder than necessary.

He pinned Brandon and Alec with a lethal stare. "Give us a minute, boys. No harm done. Mandy, would you mind getting us some glasses and that bottle of whiskey I brought along with me? I think we could all use a drink." She stood frozen, staring at him with a mixture of incredulity and arousal. "Amanda." The command in Joe's voice spurred her into action.

He held onto Caleb for another minute before asking, "We good?"

"We're good." Caleb jerked. "Get off me."

Caleb shoved Joe off his back and moved for the table. Offering Amanda his first real smile since he showed up tonight, Caleb quickly turned and crushed his right fist into Joe's face.

Joe's head was thrown to the side by the punch, but his feet stayed planted. "I see where you got your right hook, Mandy." He rubbed his jaw, moving it back and forth as if to check for damage. "I'm gonna let that one go since she's your baby sister and all."

He absently rubbed the scar along his stomach. "But don't ever try that again."

Amanda dropped the glasses she'd collected on the table with a *clank*. She glared at the men as she swiped the whiskey off the counter.

Caleb grabbed an empty glass and toasted it up. "You had it coming. And for Christ's sake, put on a fucking shirt."

"So Amanda," Alec reached for the bottle in her hand, "why

don't you sit down and tell us how Joe here became acquainted with your right hook."

"I'm much more interested in hearing how these two know each other." Amanda looked at Caleb before raising a challenging eyebrow toward Joe.

He glanced at Caleb before turning his full attention to her. "This scar you're so fascinated about, Mandy?" He accepted the full shot glass Caleb handed over and tossed it back. "The one you said looked like it was meant to gut me?" He was towering over her now and she suddenly felt weak. "Your brother is the son of a bitch who gave it to me."

CHAPTER 5

Amanda was drunk. Pleasantly numb. Warmth infused her chest as she listened to the brotherly camaraderie drifting from the foyer. Joe was at ease with her brothers, escorting them to the door as if he'd done it a hundred times. God, had she only known him a matter of hours? It felt so natural being with him. As though he'd always been here.

The night was a blur of arguments, liquor, and laughter. There was an easy acceptance of Joe that her brothers had never before exhibited with any of her other … well … men. She couldn't really call Joe her *boyfriend* now, could she?

Your brother is the son of a bitch who gave it to me.

Special Forces. Compromised mission.

Joe saved my life.

She laid her head back against her chair, pieces of the night's conversation swirling through her mind. She'd been surprised to find out Joe had been in the military, although in what capacity she still wasn't clear. She smiled slightly, thinking about her brothers' scowls when she declared that she hadn't seen any tattoos or identifying marks on Joe's body to give him away. Joe had laughed and told her she watched too many movies. And followed that up with another round of shots.

She knew better than to press for information, no matter how curious she may be. Caleb was tight-lipped about his time served. It seemed Joe was too.

Caleb had come home to take care of them after the death of their parents. Gone was the fun-loving and playful brother she knew. In his place was a hardened soldier, fierce in his protection of his family. Now, apparently, she owed her "one-night stand man" for Caleb's life. It was a little surreal.

The room spun slightly under her feet as she overheard their conversation from the other room.

"We could really use someone with your, um, skill set around the site," Brandon said.

"We're always looking for talent. From what Caleb says, you're the best," Alec added.

"I've been out for some time. I think I'll stick with the bar, but your offer is appreciated," Joe replied. She imagined them clapping each other on the back and trading handshakes.

"You're sleeping on the couch, right, Sterling?" Caleb said.

He snickered at the question. "Absolutely."

Not bloody likely.

The sky was starting to lighten. The voices faded as the men moved toward their respective rooms. They'd all had enough to drink that she'd insisted everyone stay put for the night. Or the morning, as the case may be. Her eyes drifted shut and she waited for Joe to come and take her to bed.

She came awake to Joe's breath against her cheek. "Come on, my drunk little slugger," he teased, lifting her easily into his arms. She buried her face in his neck and inhaled deeply. She felt the rumble of his laughter against her side. "Did you just smell me?"

"I did. I want to remember how delicious you smell after you're gone." He stiffened slightly as he started up the stairs. "All dark and manly." She traced the line of his jaw with her fingers. She might be hazy on the details, but one thing was for certain—Caleb had trusted this man with his life. Would she ever be willing to trust him with her heart? She snorted at the thought, causing Joe to give her a curious stare. *Get a grip, Amanda, he hasn't* asked *for your heart.*

Everyone said she gave her heart too easily. Maybe they were right. She hadn't even known Joe for twenty-four hours and already she was fantasizing about what it would be like to keep him forever. She felt a pang of regret that their time together would soon come to an end. *It's for the best.*

Her past boyfriends had bruised her pride. They'd made her question her very womanhood, but she realized now she hadn't loved them. They'd never had the power to really hurt her. This man, though—with his good looks, quick wit, and astonishing skills in the bedroom—she just knew this man was different. *I could love him. I could lose myself in him.* Meaning this man could crush her very soul. She wouldn't survive it. It wasn't a chance she could take. She'd guard her heart and enjoy him while he was here. When the time came, she'd let him go.

Joe swept her into the bedroom and she slid down his body until her feet hit the floor. She brazenly rubbed herself against his thigh and a tiny moan escaped her lips. At some point during that first bottle of Jack, she'd changed out of her robe and into her favorite yoga pants and T-shirt. The sensation of the material pressing into her aching nub was almost enough to set her off.

With a wicked gleam in her eye, she stepped back from him and slowly pulled at her T-shirt. Joe's eyes narrowed as she revealed the bare skin of her belly. She edged the shirt up to caress the bottom curve of her breasts, and then pulled it tight against her hardened nipples. "Do you have any idea what I'm thinking?" She looked pointedly at the growing bulge in his jeans.

He watched her with great interest. "I have a pretty good idea."

"You made me a promise." She moistened her lips as she sat on the end of the bed. "I aim to collect."

"Promise?" He stripped off his shirt, hardened flesh flexing with every movement.

She pouted. "You said I'd have a chance to finish you off. You wouldn't deny me, would you?"

"You're drunk." He grinned foolishly and unbuttoned his jeans.

Amanda couldn't take her eyes off his hands. Hands that had already given her more pleasure than she'd ever known. He lowered the zipper and released his cock. It bobbed against his stomach, rigid and proud. "I'm horny, that's what I am. And maybe a little drunk." She laughed lightly and looked up at him. "I want you in my mouth." She glanced down at his swollen cock. "Please."

* * *

One little word. One little word and Joe fisted his cock to stop himself from coming on the spot. This woman had him acting like a teenager the moment she got him naked.

"You are a menace," he growled.

He finished stripping off his jeans. Standing naked before her, he reached out and jerked her from the bed. His mouth came down on hers before she took a breath. He teased her with his tongue, running it lightly across the fullness of her lower lip.

"Open for me, baby," he murmured against her. "Give me what I want and I'll give you what you want."

His erection jerked against her stomach in promise. He felt her relax against him, her soft hands urgently roaming his skin. She licked and nipped at him before he took possession of her mouth. She teased the flattened disc of his nipple with her fingernail, causing his hungry male groan to fill the room.

She wanted control. It was obvious when she spun him and pushed him down onto the bed. She wore the determined look of someone with something to prove. Not to him, but to herself. He was happy to indulge her.

His cock was painfully hard. He lifted it to her in offering.

"Do you see what you do to me, Mandy? How hard I am for you? How ready I am to feel the moist heat of your sweet little mouth?" He squeezed the head, causing moisture to seep from the tip. "It's going to be so good. Fucking your mouth as you drain me. And you will drain me, won't you, Mandy? A promise is a promise."

Her cheeks darkened with lust at his words.

"You're so beautiful when you blush. How far does that blush go?" He quirked an eyebrow as he contemplated all the tempting skin beneath her clothes.

She gave him a sultry smile as she straddled his hips. "Would you like to see?" She swayed a bit as she took off her shirt and let it drift to the floor. "Oh look." She plucked at her nipples. "They're blushing too." She cupped each breast and squeezed lightly, gasping in delight at the sensation.

"Vixen," he hissed. He held her hips and pressed against her, his cock weeping for relief. She cried out as he took a rosy nipple in his mouth. "Shh, Mandy. Your brothers," he warned. He flicked his tongue over the beaded bud until she was rocking against him.

She shook her head and pushed hard against his chest. "You make me forget myself," she complained as she slid down his body again. It was all he could do to remain still as she wrapped her hand around him and squeezed. "So hot. So hard." She swiped her tongue over the tip. "So tasty."

Joe watched with lustful fascination as she ran her tongue the length of him. Heat consumed him as her fingernails raked the sensitive skin under his balls. He threaded his fingers into her hair. "That's so good, baby," he encouraged. "Take me in that sweet mouth." Her lips surrounded him, her mouth hungry and hot. Her wicked tongue teased him, flicking and lapping at the head. "Fuck." He dropped his head to the mattress as pleasure flooded his system.

He gripped her head tighter as he rocked into her. He felt the back of her throat as she struggled to take all of him. "Your mouth is so hot, Mandy." He continued to pump into her. Her cheeks were flushed as she worked him over with great enthusiasm. Her hungry eyes found his and he couldn't hold on. "Mandy," he growled as his seed blasted into her mouth. She sucked at him greedily, swallowing every last drop.

Joe shook with the force of his release. He was barely aware of the hold he'd had on her until she eased him from her mouth. He released her hair and chuckled as she swiped her tongue one last time over his tip. He collapsed back on the bed as exhaustion took over. This woman would most definitely be the death of him.

* * *

Amanda was dazed. She felt so ... so feminine. And empowered.

Joe had said her name with his release. A release she had given him. Her inhibitions fell away with the knowledge she could bring him such pleasure. Extremely satisfied, she kissed her way up his smooth, muscular chest. She lay across him and placed a chaste kiss to his lips. "Any other promises you want to make me? I find I like collecting." She nipped his neck.

His laugh was deep and husky. He tucked a stray golden curl behind her ear. "I have a promise for you, you little hellion." A warm rush of arousal flooded her pussy at the warning in his voice. "I promise I'm going to fuck you. I'm going to fuck you until you beg me for mercy."

She gasped, her inner muscles clamping down hard.

He rolled and stretched out beside her. "If you value these pants, you may want to get them off."

Amanda laughed as she hurried to comply. She felt a fluttering in her stomach as she settled beside him again.

He didn't waste any time. His fingers ran over her bare mound and he grunted in approval. "You're so wet. You must have liked sucking me. Did you, Mandy? Did you enjoy sucking my cock?" He thrust two fingers into her hungry opening.

"Joe," she moaned.

Her body clutched at him as he slowly retreated. The slick sounds of his fingers moving through her flesh echoed in the room. She arched against his hand, trying to add pressure where she needed it. His fingers sank deep, avoiding her tender nub. She bit into her forearm to keep from calling out as he stroked the sensitive spot deep in her sex. Her spine tingled as the tension continued to build. She opened her legs farther, raising her hips off the bed. She felt his fingers moving, spreading her juices before his mouth came over her. She gasped when a finger caressed the puckered opening of her ass, lightly at first, then pressing more insistently. She twisted against the surge of pleasure that pulsated from her ass to her pussy.

"Wait … Joe…" she whimpered.

She felt him press her thighs to the mattress while his sinful fingers continued to play.

"Just relax, sweetheart." Joe's voice was gentle. A low, sensual whisper. "I won't hurt you, Mandy. Don't be afraid."

Amanda couldn't fight him. She knew she should push him

away. Instead, her traitorous hips moved, straining for more. His touch was light, teasing. He circled the tiny puckered opening. The pad of his finger pressed against her, barely penetrating her outer ring. Nerve endings she didn't know existed fired lightning through her blood. She couldn't think. She felt the heat of his mouth press against her and she was lost. She was a slave to his hands, his wicked fingers that were driving her need higher and higher. She was on fire. She could feel the perspiration on her skin as she clutched at his head. She didn't know if she wanted to push him away or pull him closer.

He continued to caress her anal opening as he stroked his tongue across her swollen clit. His teeth nipped at her. She writhed beneath him, her head thrashing until her whole body came apart. Starbursts of light exploded behind her eyelids as her orgasm ripped through her. She opened her mouth in a silent scream as his tongue drove deep into her pussy, extending her pleasure until she quivered with it.

"Mercy…" she begged as he swallowed her release. "Mercy."

Her legs shook uncontrollably as she collapsed to the bed. Joe stretched out beside her. She rolled into him, curling tightly against his side. His arms came around her, surrounding her with his delicious warmth. She sighed. "I so love your promises."

He made a sound that was all satisfied, arrogant male. "Sleep," he whispered. His lips pressed against her forehead and she fell into oblivion.

Chapter 6

Joe found a stockpile of unopened toothbrushes in the bathroom and made use. His head ached, each subtle throb a reminder of why he rarely overindulged. That didn't explain the throb in his dick, though. He'd definitely overindulged with that particular part of his anatomy. It should be as limp and exhausted as the rest of him.

And yet...

He looked down at the offending organ jutting out from his stomach. He'd been disappointed to find himself alone when he woke up. His raging hard-on had been positively angry.

He smiled. Remembering her drowsy moans only rushed yet more blood to the lower part of his body. He could hear Amanda below, speaking in soft tones that soothed his nerves. He assumed she was talking to her brothers. He promised himself not to tear their heads off for putting a damper on his morning.

Ah, promises. *Damn it.*

He'd never been so attracted to anyone before. Of course, she was gorgeous. But it was more than that. She was tough, full of fire. The way she handled her brothers had him wanting to puff his chest out with a pride he had no right to feel. Not to mention the way she'd handled herself in the bar.

But she was insecure about herself. After being betrayed, not once but twice, Joe couldn't really blame her. What were those guys thinking? He wanted to track them down and beat the ever-living shit out of them for hurting her. Then thank them for being the assholes that sent her to find him. He wanted to protect her. Hell, who was he kidding? He just wanted her. The minute she'd dropped her guard and came apart in his arms he'd known.

And there was his dilemma.

One night, she'd said. *We'll just see about that.*

He went to the basket on the nightstand, grabbing several condoms and shoving them into his pocket.

As he descended the stairs, he found himself hoping Amanda was a coffee drinker. He wasn't sure he could make it through what remained of the day without a blast of caffeine. The smell of bacon drew him toward the kitchen. Amanda was dressed in his black T-shirt and from the looks of it, nothing else. He admired the long, tanned legs that disappeared beneath the hem of his shirt. Damn, she was sexy … and alone. No sign of her brothers.

"Come on, Amanda. I'm dying here," a female voice moaned from a speakerphone. "Give me something. Is he hot? He is, isn't he? Is he hung?" Her questions came like the rapid-fire of a machine gun.

Amanda laughed. "He's amazing, Sam. That's all I'm going to say so you can save your breath."

Joe was startled. He'd never been called amazing before. Well, at least not that he knew of, anyway. Hearing it from

Amanda's lips suddenly made him feel ten feet tall.

Sam evidently wouldn't give up. "He's gorgeous, right? That's why you're being so secretive."

Amanda only hummed in response.

"Hold on." Sam sounded instantly suspicious. "I know that tone."

"What tone? I didn't even say anything."

"It's what you aren't saying, Amanda."

"Stop worrying. It was fun. That's all."

Joe snorted, sensing the lie in that statement. *It was a helluva lot more than fun.*

"Uh-huh, right. So where is he now? Is he still there?"

"He's in the room," he mumbled as he walked over and wrapped his arms around Amanda's waist. He leaned in to nuzzle her neck. "Good morning, ladies," he drawled.

Amanda sank back into his chest and looked up at him.

"Mmm," she purred. "Good morning."

He nipped playfully at her earlobe. "Where are the others?"

"Gone. They had to get back."

Joe nuzzled her hair. "Hmm, that's a damn shame."

"Oh my God. Is that him?" Sam demanded from the speakerphone.

"It's him," Joe said dramatically.

"Holy shit," she groaned. "I could come from just hearing your voice. Say something else!"

"Samantha!" Amanda shrieked.

"Samantha, huh?" He kissed a path down Amanda's exposed neck. "Seems I owe you a debt of gratitude, Samantha. The gift basket was ... let's just say ... handy."

He loved how Amanda automatically tilted her head, giving him greater access. He sank his teeth into the pulse point at the base of her neck. Amanda gasped as he laved over the mark with his tongue.

Silence from the speakerphone.

"You're making breakfast." His hands caressed her bare ass and she arched into him.

"I thought you may be hungry after … well … you know." Amanda's cheeks turned a bright pink.

"If you're gonna do it…" He teased at her ear. "You might as well be able to say it. Has daylight made you shy, Mandy?"

His hand moved under the shirt. He caressed her flat belly before moving toward her breasts. He teased the curves with his fingertips. "Come on, say it," he coaxed. "After I fucked you silly." He kept his voice low, intimate. He slipped a hand between her thighs. He found her pussy wet and ready for him.

"Holy fuck," came a breathy voice from the phone.

Amanda fumbled for her phone. "I'm gonna have to call you back, Sam." She hung up without waiting to hear her reply. She turned in Joe's arms and gave him a seductive smile. "Are you hungry?"

"Starving." He reached behind her and turned off the stove. He bent down and scooped her over his shoulder.

"Joe!" Amanda laughed as she struggled to get free. "Put me down!"

There was a resounding *crack* as his hand came down on the bare cheek of her ass. Amanda gasped in shock. "Be still, you little hellion," he demanded, moving through the kitchen and into the living room. He unceremoniously dropped her onto the large leather couch. "Or I'll have to spank you again." His blood fired at the thought.

Amanda gave him a demure look. "We wouldn't want that now, would we?"

Joe narrowed his eyes before pulling the shirt over her head.

"What are you doing?" she asked.

"I'm taking my shirt back," he said simply. "You look much better without it."

* * *

Amanda shivered, the cool air causing tiny goose bumps to form on her skin. Anticipation pooled in her belly and her nipples drew up tight. She resisted the need to cover herself while Joe looked his fill.

"You are stunning." Joe's voice was a faint whisper. His eyes, darkened with desire, caressed her naked body. No one had ever looked at her that way before. Like he wanted to devour her.

Her ass tingled with warmth from his slap. She'd never been spanked before, not in discipline, not in sex. That one touch had caused a shot of lightning to surge through her ass and straight to her womb, making her clit throb with need.

Joe eased away from her and stripped off his jeans. "Do you remember last night when you mentioned making yourself come, Mandy?" His voice turned husky.

"Y-yes." Her stomach fluttered.

"Show me," he demanded.

"What?" She laughed nervously. "Now?"

"Right now." His erection was full and heavy, straining forward as if reaching for her. He palmed his length and squeezed hard. "Go on, Mandy. Touch yourself for me."

The sight of Joe gripping his own cock captivated Amanda. His hand moved with slow strokes up and down the hard flesh, precum spilling from the mushroomed head and moistening his fingers. Her mouth watered as the lips of her pussy grew wet with desire. The cool leather of the couch didn't chill the fire raging just below her skin. She was nothing but the mass of sensations that took over her body.

Slowly she brought her hands up, brushing her palms lightly across her nipples. Their gazes locked as she lightly pinched and tugged at each one. She delighted in the hitch of his breath. His shoulder rolled in subtle movement as he continued to stroke his rigid cock.

It was the most erotic thing she'd ever seen.

The lust in his eyes drove her on. Moving her hands over her stomach, she paused to draw lazy circles around her navel.

"Is this what you want?" Thrusting her breasts out, she opened her legs, exposing her wet core to his gaze. "Just having your eyes on me is making me wet, Joe. Imagining you touching me, licking me, fucking me. It's almost too much."

Amanda was stunned by the words that flowed out of her mouth. She'd never been so blatant with her sexuality, but this man brought out her inner temptress. She was no longer in control of her actions.

Joe went to his knees in front of her. His hands caressed up her legs and came to rest on her knees. He spread her wide and growled.

"More."

Amanda ran her tongue lightly over her index finger, swirling around the tip before plunging it into her mouth. She removed her finger and traced over her nipples, leaving glittering moisture behind.

"More of this?"

He dug into the skin of her thighs. "You're an evil tease."

"A tease implies you'll get no reward." She reached down and cupped her glistening pussy. "And believe me, you'll get your reward."

Her hand lowered with a quick flick of her wrist. She sucked in a breath at the pulse of electricity that sparked through her intimate folds.

She was mesmerized as Joe's tongue peeked from behind his lips. Dear God, was he panting?

She slid her finger through her wet pussy and moaned with pleasure. Joe grabbed her hand and brought it to his mouth, lightly rubbing the pad of her wet finger across his lips.

"You taste so good … so damn good. I can't wait to feel your grip around me as I fuck you." He slid her finger deep into his mouth, his tongue circling, lapping at every inch. "But first," he released her only to lean in and swipe his tongue through her slit, "you have something to show me, don't you, baby?"

How could he be so in control when she was about to come apart at the seams? It made her want to smack him.

She smiled seductively. Raising her foot to his chest, she pushed hard. Joe caught himself on his hands before he landed flat on his back. "No touching," she admonished.

"Amanda." His voice held that delicious hint of warning.

"Watch," she whispered as she ran her hands back down between her legs. Liquid heat wept from her sex, their little game making her incredibly aroused. She stretched herself open for him, running a finger around her tight opening. "Hmm, it's so hot," she teased as she eased a finger inside her slick channel, her eyes drifting shut in pleasure. She added a second finger and began a slow, torturous glide in and out.

Joe groaned loud enough to gain her attention. His balls were drawn up tight, his cock hard and ready. He reached for his discarded jeans, pulling a condom from the pocket. She moved her wet fingers over her clit as he sheathed himself.

"Look at me, Amanda," he said in a firm voice. "Look at me when you come."

Moving her fingers faster, she gazed at him. Her stomach tightened, her body coiled, preparing to release in a blast of pleasure. She screamed his name as he jerked her legs forward and entered her in one hard thrust. His groan mixed with hers as she clamped down on him and her orgasm shot through her.

He rode her slow and easy, one orgasm quickly leading to another, leaving her weak and breathless. He roared his release as she trembled around him.

Joe panted as he rested his forehead against hers. "Jesus,

that was amazing. You're amazing."

She brought his head to her chest, happy to hold his weight as she sank farther into the couch. She held him gently against her. "I've never done anything like that before." He tried to raise his head, but she held him fast.

"Regrets?" he asked.

"No, no regrets," she said, her thoughts turning sad at the thought of him leaving.

He pulled away from her, his hand cradling her cheek tenderly. "What is it, Mandy? Did I hurt you?"

"Oh, God no. Not even close. Unless you count the fact that my legs won't ever work right again," she said, her limbs quivering as she tried to squeeze him with her knees. "See?"

His eyes narrowed. "You sure?"

"Just give me a second to catch my breath and I'll finish that breakfast I started making before I was so rudely interrupted."

"Rudely interrupted?"

She winked. "When Sam called."

"Ah, right." He laughed and pushed to his feet. "How about we get some clothes on and I'll take you out for breakfast." He glanced at his watch. "Or maybe lunch."

Her stomach growled at the thought of food. "Don't you have anything else you need to do today?" She reached out her hands for him to pull her from the couch. He jerked her up, wrapping his arms around her waist and plastering her to his chest.

"You trying to get rid of me?" His lips brushed against hers.

She felt a rush of liquid between her legs as the intoxicating warmth of his skin penetrated hers. Jesus, this man could turn her into a sex addict. "Of course not, but I don't want you to feel obligated either."

His jaw twitched. "Obligated to share a meal with you?"

"You know what I mean," she said, nipping his chin.

"No, Mandy. I don't think I do." He set her on her feet, keeping his hands on her arms until she was steady.

"I just meant that if you need to be somewhere, I'd understand."

This was definitely a weird conversation to have naked, so she reached for his T-shirt and pulled it over her head. He stood watching her, arms crossed over his chest.

"What?" she asked, wide-eyed. "It's not like I have a lot of experience with the morning-after thing. I was trying to give you an out."

"I'm not looking for an out," he snapped, swiping his jeans from the floor. "I say we make our own rules."

"Really?" She didn't mean to sound so hopeful.

"Really. Jake can handle the bar. I don't have any pressing business and I'd like to spend some time with you." He stalked closer. "Unless *you* want an out."

She shook her head. "I'd like to spend some time with you too." She pressed her hands to her stomach as it grumbled again. "Starting with food." She took his hand and started from the room. She gave him a sexy smile over her shoulder. "But first we need clothes."

"You keep looking at me like that, baby, and clothes will be a long time coming," he warned, swatting her on the ass.

Her stomach clenched with a need far greater than food. She tossed him another smile. "Breakfast can wait."

Chapter 7

As far as weeks went, Samantha figured this one ranked a ten on the suck-ass scale. It wasn't so much that her apartment had been broken into. Okay, it was a little bit about that, but not as much as it was about Caleb Martin and his arrogant, dumbass idea that she couldn't take care of herself. Hell, she'd been taking care of herself for practically her whole life. Her parents sure hadn't had anything to do with it. She snorted with disgust at the thought of her mother pretending to be anything except her father's lapdog. Sit, stay, heel. Obey, obey, obey. That was all her so-called father knew, and her mother fell in line. And now it seemed Caleb was taking a page from her father's book of irritating.

What she needed was a release. Something to take her mind off all the drama that seemed to be her life lately. First her office, now her apartment. The bastard was getting desperate; she could feel it.

She eyed herself in the bathroom mirror. She'd attempted

to tame her wild mass of deep auburn curls into a subtle French braid. However, the unruly locks had a mind of their own and wisps of hair fell around her face in what she decided was sexy dishevelment. *Nothing wrong with looking a little tousled.*

Her simple black tank top was tight across her breasts, showing off just the right amount of cleavage as well as being short enough to expose the glittering gem dangling from her belly button. Her low-riding jeans only added to the wealth of toned and tanned skin she had on display. Studded rhinestones sparkled against the faded denim that trailed down into her most comfortable pair of cowgirl boots. Not her favorite choice of footwear, but this was Texas after all.

Country music drifted through the door as she leaned into the mirror to add a touch of gloss to her lips. She looked nothing like the lawyer she was, which was precisely her goal. She'd come to get her groove on and maybe to find a good-looking cowboy who wanted to join her back at the hotel she was temporarily calling home.

Pleased with her reflection, she left the bathroom and worked her way toward the bar. There were no bar stools here, only a brass rail running the length of the base for those who needed a place to rest their boots.

"Shot of tequila," she said to the bartender and slapped a twenty on the bar.

"It's on me," she heard from her left as a hand reached over and slid her money back to her.

She turned to see a very young, very handsome cowboy smiling wickedly at her. She looked him over from his black cowboy hat to his beat-up, well worn shitkickers and had to stop herself from yelling, "Jackpot!" Instead, she played it cool. "You old enough to be in here, son?" she asked.

He actually blushed and kicked his boot against the rail. Sam wouldn't have been surprised if he'd busted out with an "Aw shucks, ma'am." Instead, he just kept smiling at her. And it was quite a smile. She wondered how many panties he'd melted with that expression, because it was certainly starting to get to hers.

"I'm plenty old enough to be in here," he confirmed, leaning in to brush his lips against her ear. "But still young enough to show you a thing or two … for as long as you need showin'." He pushed his hat back on his head. "Wanna dance?" He extended his hand in offering.

She watched him as she picked up her shot glass and brought it to her lips. His golden gaze was glued to her mouth as she licked the rim slightly before drinking it down in one gulp. When she reached to take his hand, he swooped his arm around her and lifted her off her feet, pressing her tight against him.

"Oh!" She laughed as he swung her around and placed her on her feet again. "Please tell me that wasn't it."

"We're just gettin' started, darlin'. I aim to burn off a little steam tonight, and you're just about the tastiest thing I've ever seen. Care to join me in a little hell-raisin'?"

"Cowboy, you have no idea. Buy me another shot and then you can show me your moves," she said suggestively and smiled as he threw his head back in laughter.

He twirled his finger at the bartender to signal another round. "Darlin', I got moves that'll curl your toes," he promised.

"I'm counting on that, Cowboy," she said as she accepted her drink.

After another round, she was beginning to feel the blissful warmth that came with being tipsy. She was far from drunk and perfectly happy to let her cowboy lead her to the dance floor. She pressed herself along the length of him and swayed as he spun her into a slow, tight dance. His hands caressed the skin of her back, farther exposed as she reached up and laced her fingers around his neck.

Halfway through the first song they were interrupted by

another man looking to cut in. Cowboy clutched her tight for a minute and put his mouth to her ear. "I don't mind watching you dance with other guys tonight, darlin', but you're goin' home with me." He winked at her before giving her ass a possessive squeeze and passing her to the other man.

After Sam had danced with just about every guy in the place, she felt as if she was going to fall over. She laughingly held off her next admirer. "I need a drink." Her buzz was completely gone. She scanned the crowd for Cowboy and found him watching her from the spot at the bar where they'd met. He held up a glass to her to indicate he had one waiting.

The minute she reached him, he grabbed her up and planted a kiss on her lips. She opened and let him in. And boy oh boy, he didn't disappoint. His lips were firm and demanding. His mouth possessed her; his tongue tangled with hers until she was breathless. She pulled away. "What was that for?" she asked.

"Because you're drivin' me crazy, that's why." He nuzzled her cheek.

His hand caressed up her side, his thumb grazing intimately across her nipple. Her body responded immediately, her nipples tightening into hard buds and warmth flooding her panties. "You about ready to get out of here?" she asked.

"Finish your drink, darlin', then I'll take you wherever you wanna go." He reached down and lightly fingered the jewel at her navel. "'Cause honestly, I can't wait to get you naked."

Oh hell yeah!

She pressed her breasts against his chest and nipped his chin. "And what'll do you with me once you get me naked?"

"He's not going to do a goddamned thing, because he's not getting you naked," a voice growled from behind her.

"What's it to you?" Her cowboy sneered over her shoulder. "You her boyfriend or somethin'?"

"Or something," Sam said as a hand clamped down on

her bicep. She didn't turn around, just glared at the fingers that gripped her. "Get your hand off me, Caleb." She jerked her arm, emphasizing her demand.

"Mister, I don't know who the hell you are, but the lady doesn't want you touching her so how's about you back the fuck off?"

"*Son*, unless you want a whole mess of shit you can't handle, which in my current mood would suit me just fine, *you'll* back the fuck off. Trust me when I say I could wipe the floor with you without breaking a sweat." His grip increased on Sam's arm. "Wanna try me?"

Sam gave her cowboy a defeated look. "I'm sorry. This isn't what I intended. This jackass," she tugged on her arm again, "thinks he's some kind of watchdog or something. Maybe we can hook up … hey!" Caleb jerked her back against him.

"She's nothing but trouble, I assure you. Get out while the gettin's good, man." Caleb sounded almost apologetic.

Sam nodded at her cowboy and he backed off. "I ain't lookin' for a fight, dude. I was just lookin' to have some fun. If she's yours, then by all means. But you really should keep a better eye on her. A gal like her won't ever be alone long." He winked at her before strolling off and leaving her in Caleb's clutches.

Un-fucking-believable.

"Let go of me, Caleb." Her hands itched with the urge to slug him.

"Are you going to be good?"

Seriously? "No."

"Then what's my incentive to let go?" He pulled her deeper into his chest, sounding as close to being amused as she'd ever heard him.

"Um, keeping your balls in their proper anatomical position?"

He snorted. "We're going to talk, Samantha."

She whirled on him, forcing him to release her or twist her arm. He quickly released her. "No." She jabbed her finger into his chest. "You mean you're going to talk and you expect me to listen. Who do you think you are, anyway? You've never given two shits about me or my life except when it concerns Amanda. Now that you know where she is, there shouldn't be any reason for you to keep hounding me."

"For some ungodly reason," he took hold of her arm again, "everything about you concerns Amanda." He gave her a pointed stare. "Which concerns me."

She dug her boot heels into the floor as he started to drag her away. "I'm not leaving."

"You're not staying." He simply continued to pull her along behind him.

She cursed and followed, if only to save herself the embarrassment of tripping and being dragged out of the bar on her ass. By the time they hit the parking lot, she was steaming mad. And still very horny.

He backed her up to his truck and was in her face before she could form words to yell at him. "Just what the fuck did you think you were doing in there?" he demanded.

Sam was taken aback by the anger rolling off him. Oh sure, he'd been mad at her in the past. Hell, she wouldn't know what to do if he wasn't frustrated with her about something. But this was new. She'd never seen him actually ready to spit nails at her before. She wasn't sure what to do. Flustered, she pushed at him. He didn't budge so much as an inch.

Bastard.

"Do you have any idea who broke into your office? Your apartment?" She opened her mouth to respond but he kept going. "How do you know that whoever is looking for you isn't in this bar right now? That he isn't that innocent-looking cowboy you almost took back to your hotel? Christ, Samantha, you can't be this foolish."

"I'm not being foolish, I was trying to get laid. Burn off a little stress, you know?" She sneered at him. "You ought to try it. It might help your disposition a little."

"You offering? 'Cause I guarantee I could do a better job than the youngster you were about to leave with." His eyes flashed in a way that made her suddenly uneasy.

She took a breath. "You're such an ass."

"Tell me something I don't already know, darlin'. But that doesn't change the fact that someone is looking for you, or something you have. Until we figure this out, you've got to be more careful. No more bars, no more … well, just no more."

The command in his voice pissed her off. He was ordering her around like her father had tried to do, and that was something she wouldn't stand for.

"For the last time, Caleb, I can take care of myself. I know who's looking for me, and I know what they're looking for."

He jerked away from her, his face as hard as granite. "Who?"

She sighed and pushed at him again, this time successfully gaining some breathing room as he took a step back from her. "The husband of a client." She gave him a weary look and decided to give him a taste of the truth. "I helped her get away. He's powerful, Caleb, but he won't get what he wants from me. Ever."

"What does he want?" His voice shook with barely controlled anger.

"He wants his wife."

"And this wife … she's worth putting yourself at risk?"

Sam couldn't believe he'd asked her that question. "He almost killed her, Caleb." She considered him hard. "You'd have me send her back to save my own skin?" She was mortified he believed she'd do such a thing.

He didn't hesitate. "Yes." He blew out a harsh breath. "No."

He shook his head. "Of course not. But there has to be another way, goddammit."

"I'm working on it. It's not like they've threatened my life or anything. Living in a hotel is a small price to pay to keep my client safe. I get my meals cooked for me and have clean towels every morning," she said, making light of the situation.

"They?" He got in her face again. *"They?"*

"I can only assume this man wouldn't want to dirty his own hands. I'm speculating here, but I'd say he'd hire men to do things like break into my apartment."

"And these hired men, to what lengths will they go to obtain the information they want?"

"Now, how the hell am I supposed to know that? But again, it doesn't matter. There's nothing to find. The only way to get the information is to get it from me. And I'm. Not. Talking." She jabbed her finger into his chest with each word.

He stiffened. "Give me a name."

"This isn't your fight."

He let loose a string of vile curses. "Give me the name, Samantha."

"Forget it. Look, I'll be good and go back to my hotel, but only because I'm tired of standing here fighting with you. I won't go back in the bar and I won't take anyone back to the hotel with me." She let her frustration show as she pushed past him and headed for her car. "But I'm damn sure going to stop at the nearest adult toy store on my way," she tossed over her shoulder. "Since you ruined any chance I had of having a real cock in my henhouse tonight, I'll at least have a fucking artificial replacement."

* * *

Caleb cursed as he watched Samantha walk away. He had no desire to watch her go shopping for her battery-operated boyfriend, but he wasn't going to let her out of his sight. At least until she was safe at her hotel. It's what he did. He kept his family safe, and like it or not, Samantha was family. According to Amanda, anyway.

He climbed into the cab of his truck and pulled out his cell. He punched the numbers and listened as the internal speaker system took over the call.

"'Sup, bro?" Brandon's voice greeted him.

"Hey, I need you guys to do something for me." He was walking a fine line with this one and he knew it.

"Hang on." He heard Brandon switch to speakerphone. "Alec," he yelled. "C'mere."

"What's all the yelling about?" Alec was panting as if he'd run from another part of the building or something.

"Caleb's on the line."

"Hey Alec. I'm glad you're both there. I could really use both of you, but mostly you, Alec." He heard Brandon snort as if he'd just been told he was the consolation prize.

"You know I got mad skills," Alec joked. "What's up?"

Caleb pulled into traffic, keeping Samantha within his sights as he thought about how to best go about asking for what he needed.

"Caleb?"

"Yeah, Bran. I'm here, sorry. Listen, I need you guys to come up with a list of Samantha's clients for the past couple of years." He waited for them to start yelling at him about confidentiality and the repercussions of breaking into her client list, but all he heard was silence. "Guys?"

"Wanna explain that?" Alec asked. "I mean, if I'm gonna break the law, I want a good reason."

"She just told me that she knew who broke into her office and her apartment." He heard the sharp intake of breath from the other end of the line as he kept talking. "And she knows what they were looking for. When I questioned her about it, all she'd say was that it was the husband of a client she'd helped. A very powerful husband," he emphasized. "Since we handle all of her IT security, it's not technically illegal if you stumble across client names while you're backing things up, right?" He was reaching.

"Hold up, just what's she gotten herself into?" Brandon asked.

Caleb could hear fingers flying across a keyboard. "I have no idea. That's what I need you for. I'd do it myself, but I'm better with the tactical stuff. Plus, I can't leave Samantha unprotected until we figure this out."

"Right, like following her around is such a hardship, huh, Cay?"

"Bite me, Alec," Caleb said dryly as he pulled up to the adult store and watched her flounce inside. Would she really buy a vibrator in there? What else would she come out with? He cleared his throat. "Once we have a name, Amanda can run a background check. That should give us a starting point."

"Wouldn't it just be easier to talk to Sam?" Brandon was always the most logical one.

"You'd think, wouldn't you?" The sarcasm dripped from Caleb's voice. "Sam's not talking."

"Maybe not to you," Alec interjected, "but she might talk to one of us. Maybe Amanda?"

"Doubtful," Caleb said. "She's determined to prove she can take care of herself. She made it clear she doesn't want us involved."

"So, of course, we're getting involved." Brandon laughed.

"Of course," Caleb grunted as he watched Samantha walk back out of the store with a brown paper sack in her hand. She smiled and waved the bag at him right before getting into her car, indicating she knew he was following her. His mind was racing with the possibilities of what was in that sack.

Holy shit, why do I even care?

"Call me when you have it narrowed down," Caleb said. "Get me that name. Then I'll call Amanda and get the ball rolling. Maybe by then Samantha will be more cooperative." He highly doubted it, though. They said quick good-byes and Caleb disconnected the call.

As he followed her back to the hotel, he couldn't stop thinking about her and that damn sack. Or more importantly, what was in the sack. Maybe Samantha was right. Maybe it was time he got laid.

Chapter 8

Four days. Amanda stared aimlessly out the window. Four blissful days.

I'm in serious trouble.

The time she'd spent with Joe made her yearn for something more. He seemed genuinely interested in her, listening attentively as she spoke and, at night, never leaving her unsatisfied. He was sexy and laid-back, content to just hang with her around the ranch.

He'd held her hand as they walked her property, curious about her life here. She'd delighted in the feel of his warm hand engulfing hers while she'd explained that her father had planted the orchard because her mother loved to bake with fresh fruit. What she didn't use, she gave away. Her mother had reasoned that the fruit was cultivated for her own pleasure and not for resale value. *"The only thing sadder than waste,"* she remembered her mother saying, *"is someone trying to profit from it."*

"What happens to the fruit now that no one lives here?" Joe

had thoughtfully asked her.

Amanda didn't know. Caleb had taken responsibility for this and other properties her parents had owned prior to their deaths. She'd made a mental note to find out. He'd seen to it that the house was well cared for. Although there were no more animals here, the stable and barn were still standing and in excellent condition. She could only assume he wouldn't let their mother's beloved fruit go to waste. She said as much as they walked among the trees, the lingering smell of apples bringing a smile to her face.

She'd taken him to the corral. As he perched on the fence rail, a lazy smile on his face, she'd dramatically reenacted the first time she'd been thrown from a horse. As a reward for her performance, he'd fucked her fast and hard against the stable doors. And again in the barn. She giggled at the thought of leaving a trail of condom wrappers, like bread crumbs, to show where they'd been.

In the evenings they'd cooked dinner together. Joe turned out to be quite handy in the kitchen. He was excellent at fetching this pan or that spoon. She also found he was quite efficient with stirring things while keeping most of the contents in the pan. After they ate, Joe would pour her a glass of wine while splashing whiskey into a glass for himself, and they'd sit together on the porch swing. They'd talked as the sun set and the stars shone in the sky. She'd made him laugh with stories of growing up with three older brothers. He'd surprised her with stories of all the beautiful places he'd seen. He'd wrapped his arms around her to warm her against the cool evening breeze that always seemed to blow this time of year. They lapsed into comfortable silence, and the night would begin to take over.

They'd made out like teenagers in front of the fireplace before he'd made love to her over and over. The man gave stamina a whole new meaning.

Yep, I'm in real trouble.

She loved that he couldn't keep his hands off her. She loved that he was demanding and fierce one minute, romantic and sweet the next. She loved … *no, no, no. Not going there.* She hadn't even known him a full week. There was no way … *dammit.*

Turning back to her desk, Amanda opened her laptop. Just thinking about Joe had made her wet and needy. He'd gone out for a run, and she didn't know how long she had before he returned. Her heart raced with excitement. He'd come in sweaty and energized. Hmm, it seemed he wasn't the only one who couldn't get enough.

She opened her e-mail program. Caleb had demanded she check in daily while she was here and she'd agreed, if only to shut him up. She drafted a quick e-mail letting him know she was okay and on track to return to work at the start of the week. Just the thought of leaving made her sick to her stomach. She'd forgotten how much she loved this place, this land. And now with Joe here, well, all the more reason for her to want to stay. Not that she was entertaining any thought at all about having a relationship with him. They were just having fun. A hot guy like him would have a whole string of women waiting for him, and she was tired of sharing.

Her cell phone rang. Caleb.

"Hi, Cay. I just sent you a message," she said cheerfully.

"I got it, thanks. It'll be great to have you back in the office. How are things there?"

She laughed at how casual he sounded. "Things are fine here. You need something?"

"That transparent, huh?"

"Spit it out."

"I need you to run a background check. Hold up," he said as she started to speak, "before you bombard me with a hundred questions, get a pen and write this down. Name is Vincent

Matteo. He's some New York corporate bigwig. Investment banker. His last known residence is Manhattan. I need a full workup." When she didn't say anything he added, "Now would be good."

Interesting. "What are you looking for ... specifically?" Her brain immediately reverted to work mode. "You know better than to give me such a broad scope. I'll be running blind without some kind of idea of what you're looking for, Cay. I'm not willing to waste weeks on irrelevant information." She was already running search scenarios in her head.

"Last-known whereabouts is priority."

"What does he drive?"

"Maserati."

"Of course he does," Amanda said. "'Cause what else would a guy named Vincent Matteo drive?"

Caleb barked out a rare laugh. "I'll text you the license plate number once I have it."

"Great. Anything else?"

"Financial transactions, legal troubles, relationships, offshore bank accounts ... anything you can find."

"I don't suppose you're going to tell me what this is about?"

"Nope."

Typical. Amanda sighed. "I'll do what I can and get back to you. Depending on if he's trying to lay low, finding him shouldn't be much trouble. He's in the country, right?"

"Most definitely." Caleb sounded as if he already knew where the guy was.

"Is he trying to lay low?"

"That's what I'd like to know," Caleb mumbled.

Very interesting.

They said their good-byes and Amanda got to work. After an hour she'd learned more than she wanted to know about this guy. Vincent Matteo was indeed a corporate hotshot with political ties that ran deep. She found a string of corruption charges, but none that ever stuck. There were even reports that he had ties to a NYC crime family, although she could find no evidence linking him to any illegal activity … yet. His wife had mysteriously disappeared over a year ago. According to local papers, he'd been devastated. A reward was being offered for information leading to her recovery, dead or alive. *What was Caleb doing?*

"Mandy?" Joe's voice called from the front room. "Baby, where are you?"

She was still tracking the license plate Caleb had texted her, but it would take a while. No need to babysit the screen. "I'm coming," she called brightly.

"We have company," he called back to her.

Her heart skipped a beat. *We.* He said it so casually. As though they were a couple or something. She walked into the living room to see Sam standing next to him. "Sam! What are you doing here?" Amanda walked straight into Joe's arms. She stood on her tiptoes and nuzzled his neck, inhaling his manly scent.

"Mandy," Joe chastised, "I'm all sweaty." He gave her a quick squeeze and gently set her from him. "Company," he reminded her as he turned her to face Sam.

Her best friend was studying her.

"What?" Amanda asked.

Sam rolled her eyes. "Nice to see you too." Amanda approached as if to hug her, but Sam held her off. "Oh no you don't. Now *you're* all sweaty."

"Ha-ha." Amanda put her hands on her hips. "Not that I'm not glad to see you, but seriously, what are you doing here?"

"I came to see how you were faring." Sam gave Joe the once-over. "After that phone call the other day, how could I not?" She winked at him.

Amanda felt a surge of anger as she watched her friend eat up her lover with her eyes. She stepped in her line of vision. "Seen enough?" *God, when did I get so possessive?*

Sam's eyes widened in surprise. "Take it easy, killer. Just checking out the scenery." Amanda didn't know what Sam saw in her face just then, but she suddenly looked hurt. "Really, Amanda?"

Joe laughed and wrapped his arm around Amanda. "Why don't you girls grab some wine and talk while I get cleaned up. Then I'll make us all something to eat. It'll give me and Samantha a chance to get acquainted."

Amanda looked skeptical. "You're going to cook?"

"Hey!" He put his hand over his heart. "You wound me. I can open and heat with the best of them." He winked at her and placed a kiss on her forehead. "I promise it'll be great. You're just gonna have to trust me."

Amanda leaned into him. "You know how I love your promises."

His eyes flared with lust. "Oh, I haven't even begun to make you promises, baby," he whispered so only she could hear. He looked at her and then at Sam and back to her. "Right." He gently pushed Amanda away, his look warning her he'd make good ... later. "Go talk. I need a shower." He took the steps two at a time, mumbling something about getting the water cold enough.

"What the hell?" Sam lit into her the moment Joe was out of sight.

Amanda rubbed her hand over her face. This was her best friend. The last person in the world who would ever try to hurt her. "Ah, jeez. I'm sorry, Sam. I don't know what got into me."

Sam crossed her arms defensively and motioned for her to go on.

"It's just that you're the one with the fire-red hair and rockin' body. Not me." Amanda grinned sheepishly. "I'd like to hang on to his attention for a little longer, if you don't mind."

"I'll not argue about my rockin' body," Sam joked with a wink, "but honey, that man wouldn't have noticed me if I'd run in here naked and slicked up with baby oil. Not with you in the room."

"Yeah, right."

"Holy shit, girl. Are you kidding me? I don't think a man has ever looked at me like that."

"Like what?"

"Like Joe looks at you. I mean really, Amanda. He looks at you like he's ... like he's ... I don't know ... *hungry.*"

Amanda blushed to her toes. "As much as we've ... well, he shouldn't be hungry." Amanda laughed, urging Sam toward the couch. "Get comfy. I'll grab us a bottle of wine."

When she reentered the living room, she found Sam curled up on one end of the couch, her legs drawn up to her chest. "You okay?" Amanda sank into the other end of the couch and faced her.

Sam jumped at the sound of Amanda's voice. *What the hell?* Sam was never jumpy.

"I'm sorry for barging in on your weeklong sexfest, Amanda. I just needed to get away for a bit. I hope you don't mind."

Amanda handed her the wine bottle. Screw the glasses. As if on cue, Sam raised the bottle to her lips and drank. And drank. And drank.

"Whoa there, slow down." Amanda grabbed the bottle. "First off, of course it's okay that you're here. To be honest, I could use a little female company. Not that I've minded the male company I've had." She wagged her eyebrows suggestively.

"So, about that." Sam hiccupped lightly. "Do tell. And don't leave anything out. He's as hot as a firecracker. And aren't those just the bluest eyes you've ever seen? Is he as hot in the sack?"

"Sam!"

"Well? I gotta get my rocks off somehow! Might as well live vicariously through you.

"What are you talking about? Since when do you live like a nun?"

"Since your brother—" She stopped abruptly, clamping her lips shut so tight they turned white.

Amanda gasped. "You didn't?" She took a long draw from the bottle. "Please tell me you didn't."

Sam snorted with disgust. "Of course I didn't. Why on earth would I want to sleep with the most annoying, arrogant, self-centered, egotistical—"

"All right, all right." She passed the bottle back. "I get it." *I don't get it.* "What's he done now?" She suddenly wished she'd grabbed something stronger than wine.

The floodgates opened on a string of curse words. "Why he thinks it's his right to watch over me just pisses me off. I can't go anywhere, do anything without him right there … watching, hovering. I mean really, Amanda, would *you* go home with me if you had to go through Caleb to do it? I'm about at my wit's end … and not just because I can't get laid."

Amanda was so confused. Maybe it was the wine. "Tell me again why Caleb is following you? Why in the hell would Caleb follow you?" She wasn't sure if she was asking Sam or herself.

Sam was quiet for a long time. Amanda watched her carefully as they passed the bottle back and forth. She knew an explanation would come, but it would be on Sam's terms. As was everything else in Sam's life. Amanda suspected that was the reason she and Caleb were at each other's throats all the time. Two control freaks vying to be the one in control. It was a recipe for disaster.

Finally Sam spoke. "You remember that case I took last year? The woman I helped get a divorce after her husband beat her to within an inch of her life?"

Amanda remembered. It was a particularly brutal case that had tied her best friend in knots. Amanda had helped Sam secure a new identity for the woman so she could relocate and try to rebuild her life. Of course, Sam hadn't divulged any of the details. Just that the woman's life was in danger and she needed a new start. "Sure I do. What does that have to do with Caleb?"

"The husband has been around," Sam said simply.

Amanda eyed her suspiciously. "Around … how?"

Sam shrugged. "Can't prove anything. Remember when someone broke into my office?"

"Of course I do." Amanda had demanded Caleb allow Sam to move her office into their building because of it.

"The divorce file was the only one missing," Sam continued. "It's a good thing I'm not that stupid."

Amanda gave her a puzzled look.

"I didn't leave a paper trail, Amanda. I was careful in relocating Matteo's wife. Her life depended on it. He can look all he wants; he won't find anything." Sam uttered a tired sigh. "But apparently he's not done looking because my apartment was ransacked. I crashed at Alec's, who, of course, blabbed to Caleb. Caleb was furious that someone got into my building, although I can't even begin to imagine why." Sam slumped back into the arm of the couch. "I'm not real happy about any of it either. Caleb and I had a fight … in a bar, no less. I know"—she rubbed her forehead—"imagine that, right? I came clean about how I helped the wife. I learned a few words I'd never heard before during *that* conversation." She smiled slightly. "Don't worry. I left you out of it. There's no way anyone will find out you helped me, not even Caleb."

Matteo. "Wait." Amanda's mind was racing. "Wait just a goddamn minute. Matteo? As in *Vincent* Matteo? Corporate tycoon? The Vincent Matteo whose fingers are into everything from governmental policy to a possible tie to the *mob*?" Amanda could feel her voice rising. Okay, so she knew the mob thing wasn't substantiated, but still. "*That's* the wife-beater who got off because evidence was *accidentally* lost? *That's* the man you suspected had bribed a guy inside the police department?" Sam's eyes narrowed on her, but she didn't care. "Are you telling me that this is the same guy who's trying to get to you now?"

"How do you know about all of that?" Sam demanded. Another string of curses flowed from Sam's mouth. "Caleb."

"He called me this afternoon and asked me to do a background check. Didn't tell me why. You connected the dots when you said his name."

Sam didn't say anything as she reached for her cell. She tapped her fingers against her leg as she put the phone to her ear and waited. Amanda assumed it was Caleb who'd answered when Sam yelled, "Who the fuck do you think you are? Having your sister run a background check?" A moment passed. "What do you mean how do I know about that? I'm sitting directly across from her! No, she's not home, I'm at Fawn Glade. Don't you dare act all relieved to know where I am, you fucking bastard. Did you have someone hack into my goddamn client list?"

Amanda shook her head as Sam shot her an accusatory glare. "Wasn't me," she mouthed.

Sam growled into the phone. "You're not my brother or my father, nor are you my husband. I don't have to tell you shit." Another moment. "Mind your own fucking business, Caleb. This doesn't have anything to do with you." Amanda watched as Sam's face paled slightly. "No, I wasn't fucking followed. Yes, I'm sure! I'd never—" Sam paled further as she listened into the phone. "Fine. I'll come back tonight, but I'm going to a hotel. No. Absolutely not. Hotel, period. End of discussion. Whichever one I want to stay in, that's where!" Another pause, and then, "Go to hell, horseman." She ended the call and tossed her phone on the table.

"What's all the yelling about?" Joe strode into the room, looking incredibly sexy in his jeans and bare feet. Amanda's mouth watered as he ran his fingers through his wet hair.

"Sam was talking to Caleb."

"Ah." As if that was all that was needed to explain the yelling. "I don't know about you girls, but I'm not drinking wine. How about something a little stronger to warm your bellies?"

* * *

Dinner wasn't quite the disaster Amanda thought it would be. She and Sam sat at the table while Joe informed them that, yes, even he could boil water. Sam had brought in a bottle of rum and offered to share. Amanda and Joe declined, opting for beer instead. Amanda had no intention of getting drunk tonight. She wanted to be at full capacity for whatever Joe had planned for her. If the looks he kept sending her way were any indication, it was going to be good.

His cell phone rang, surprising her. He glanced at it and with a terse "Excuse me, ladies," he was gone. It was the first time since she'd known him that it had rung. It made her curious. Curious about his life. About who'd be calling him. If it was a woman that was calling him. Thoughts like that could drive a girl nuts.

"I hope *Italiano* for dinner works for both of you," he said as he sauntered back into the kitchen a few minutes later, entertaining them with his best Italian accent. "It's about all I can do." He gave no indication as to the conversation he'd just had.

"How did you learn to do that so well?" Sam asked.

"Cook pasta?"

"No, smart-ass. The accent."

"It's sexy," Amanda threw in before she could slam her

mouth shut. Joe gave her a look that would melt the clothes off a saint.

"Uh, guys?" Sam waved her hand in front of Amanda's face. "Company, remember?"

Amanda swigged from her beer and smirked. "Can you blame me? I mean ... *look* at him." She gestured in his direction with her bottle. She blocked her mouth with her hand so Joe wouldn't see. "Isn't he fantastic?" she mouthed to Sam, happy they were okay after her stellar performance of a jealous bitch.

Sam giggled back at her. "So, Mr. Hot Stuff—"

"Name's Joe. Not 'Mr. Hot Stuff,'" he grumbled, which just set off another round of giggles from Sam.

"The accent?"

He shrugged. "Spent some time in Italy a few years back."

"What on earth were you doing in Italy?"

Joe gave Sam a droll stare. "Shopping."

"Riiiight," she said as she winked at Amanda. "Shopping. I'll bet you bought the greatest shoes, didn't you?"

He chuckled and shook his head. "No shoes, but I got a great pair of boots I can introduce you to."

She laughed again. "I like him, Amanda. He's got spunk."

"I like him too," Amanda said with way more feeling than she'd intended. *Oops.* She noted the curious way Joe stared at her before turning back to the stove.

"I met this old Italian woman in Trieste who took pity on me," he said. "I think she thought I'd starve if she didn't take me in and feed me enormous amounts of food." His face took on a gentle expression. "She told me that if a man only knew how to cook one thing, it should be pasta. So she taught me."

"Trieste? Never heard of it," Sam said.

"It's on the eastern border," he returned casually.

"The border of Slovenia?" Amanda asked as her brain sifted through the geography.

He shot her a warning look. "Let's eat."

"Wow, touchy," Sam observed.

Amanda nodded in agreement, but they both let it go.

"So, Joe," Sam started after they'd settled in to eat, "you from around here?"

"For the most part, yes. I grew up here."

"And your parents?"

He shook his head. "Just me and Jake."

"Jake?"

"Younger brother," Amanda added for him. "He's cute too."

"Interesting," Sam said smoothly, "I've always liked the young ones. Any chance of an introduction?"

"I'm not Jake's pimp." Joe acted offended, but Amanda could tell by the humor in his eye that he liked Sam's candor.

"You told Caleb you were headed back tonight," Amanda reminded gently.

Sam's eyes blazed. "Wouldn't wanna disappoint the horseman now, would I?" She looked at Amanda. "Why the hell is he on my ass all of a sudden?" When Amanda didn't offer a response, she continued. "Let's see how much sleep he gets tonight as he searches every last hotel to find me. Hmm, maybe I'll check in under a different name." Her smile was pure evil.

"Caleb is right, Sam," Joe said.

Her gaze snapped to his. "What do you know about it?"

He pushed his plate away with a sigh. Leaning back in his chair, he crossed his arms over his chest as he considered her. "Enough to know you're foolish to play with your own life." He shrugged at her questioning gaze. "He called me. He sounded … concerned." Amanda tried not to look relieved to learn it had been Caleb on the phone.

Sam made an unladylike sound. "He called you because he's concerned I let the douche bag follow me to his precious sister. As if I'd ever willingly put Amanda in danger. Asshole."

He nodded. "True enough, but he knows you're both safe with me."

Sam eyed him cautiously. "And just who are you?"

"As crazy as this sounds, Joe and Caleb know each other." Amanda watched as Sam digested this new tidbit of information.

Sam just looked defeated. "Of course. What are the odds?" she whispered to herself. "The fourth horseman," she said ironically. "Look, Amanda." She waved her hand absently at Joe. "Now we have the whole set. Four impossibly arrogant males who think they always know best."

Joe raised a brow at Amanda. She shook her head in that "don't ask" kind of way.

"So you're taking his side?"

"This isn't about sides, Samantha. But if it were, I'm firmly on the side that keeps you safe. Caleb can do that."

I know he can do it," she snapped, "he's just so annoying about it." She slid her rum and Coke across the table. "Fine. Better serve up some fucking coffee if I'm going to make the drive back tonight."

* * *

Joe was wound tighter than a drum as they stood on the porch and watched Samantha drive off. Once the coffee had been made, Amanda had brought out some cards and the three of them played several of the most enjoyable games of poker he'd ever been a part of. Those girls took cheating to a whole new level. He'd never laughed so hard in his life. That was until Amanda threw herself into his lap and kissed him stupid while Samantha attempted to trade cards with him. He couldn't have cared less about the cards, but his dick was all about caring that Amanda was in his lap and in his mouth. He took little satisfaction in the fact that she seemed as dazed as he was after she slid back into her own chair. Mainly because she'd left him with an erection so hard he could have driven nails with it.

She turned him on even when she wasn't trying. When she chewed on her bottom lip while thinking, it reminded him of how she did the same thing when she was about to come. She'd carelessly throw him a wink, tossing her ponytail teasingly when she was about to either steal money from Samantha's pile or slide a card under the deck. Or she pretended to stretch, pointing her delicious breasts right at him as a distraction. So yeah, he was about to shoot off like a firecracker.

They walked back in the house together and Joe closed and locked the door.

"I guess I better get to those dishes." Amanda started for the kitchen. "Dinner was great, by the way."

"Don't. Move." His demand froze her feet in place. He circled before crowding her back into the door. He crushed his mouth to hers in a brutal kiss. She yelped at the onslaught, but quickly got with the program. She wrapped her arms around his neck and pulled him closer. He devoured her, ate at her, licked at her until they were both breathless. He pulled back and narrowed his eyes on her. "Strip."

"But—"

"Now, Amanda." His command left no room for argument. "I want you right. Fucking. Now."

Her hands were shaking as they moved to the button of her jeans. In a matter of seconds she stood gloriously naked in front of him. He drank her in. Her eyelids were heavy with desire. The delicate pink of her tongue teased him as she licked her lips. Her ponytail exposed the long line of her neck. Her nipples were standing hard and proud, the rose-colored pebbles just begging for his attention. He smiled, watching the firm muscles of her stomach twitch under his gaze. The bare lips of her pussy glistened with her excitement. *Perfection.*

"Turn around," he growled. He didn't wait for her to obey

his command but grabbed her bicep and spun her. He rested his forearm against the door and pushed his body into hers. He felt her shudder as her forehead came to rest on his arm. He wrapped his hand around her ponytail and pulled her head back. "You make me crazy, Mandy. Do you have any idea how sexy you are? The way your tongue plays with the rim of your beer bottle as you take a drink. The way your lips wrapped around your fork as you ate." He dropped his forehead on her shoulder. "The way you chew on that fucking lip." He groaned. "Every move you make drives me absolutely bat-shit crazy."

The sound of a zipper releasing filled the room. He pushed at her feet. "Spread wider for me, baby. That's it. Open those legs for me. I won't go slow, Mandy. Once I get inside you … I won't go slow." He leaned in and trailed his tongue down the sensitive skin behind her ear. "And I won't settle for just once." Her moan filled his ears as she pressed back against him.

His hand connected with her ass with a loud *crack*. "Don't move."

"Hey!" Her startled cry made him smile. She struggled to get away.

His palm met with her wet folds in a quick, sharp slap. Amanda went stiff. Her throat rumbled with a sexy little laugh as she rubbed her ass against his groin again.

"Stop." He ground his palm against her sweet spot.

She was panting. "You aren't giving me much incentive to stop," she said seductively. "Spank me again." She wiggled her ass at him.

"Damn sassy woman." *Mine.* He latched onto the base of her neck and sucked hard. Her head fell to the side. "I can make this go on all night, sweetheart. I can drive you higher and higher, keeping you on the edge without ever letting you over." He put his mouth to her ear. "You want to come, don't you, baby?"

Amanda stilled under his hands. "That's a good girl. You

should see how pretty your ass looks right now, Mandy. All pink and warm." He caressed both cheeks before connecting again with two hard spanks. He smiled to himself as he saw her toes curl against the floor with her effort to remain still. Her breath was coming in short gasps, and then stopped altogether as he rubbed his erection against the crack of her ass, sliding down to her wet core. "Breathe, Mandy," was the only warning she got before he shifted and slammed into her.

She cried out and his control was shot. Over and over he pounded into her. His fingers dug into the flesh of her hips, but he couldn't force himself to let go. She leaned forward, giving him greater access. He took total advantage, burying himself to the hilt in her tight grip.

"Joe, please," she begged.

"Tell me what you need, baby."

"Harder. Faster."

He wrapped his arm around her waist and lifted her feet off the floor. He turned them around to the rug that spanned the entryway floor. "Hands and knees," he demanded as he dropped them to the floor, all the while remaining lodged inside her. "Brace yourself." He grabbed her shoulders and began to pound into her once again. He felt her tense just moments before crying out her pleasure. His balls drew up tight the second she clamped down on him. He swore as he exploded into her, pulse after pulse of hot semen erupting from him as he filled her channel. A wave of dizziness overcame him. He kept moving, his hips having a mind of their own, every thrust prolonging their shared pleasure.

Finally he slowed. "Damn," was all he could manage as he fought to catch his breath.

Amanda's body gave out and she face-planted into the floor. Her voice was muffled from the rug. "That ... wow. That was the most amazing, most incredible sex I've ever experienced."

Joe resisted the urge to pound his chest like a damn caveman. He gently pulled out of her. "Shit, Mandy…" He sat back on his haunches as she languidly stretched and sat up to face him. "I don't know what happened. I forgot. I never forget." He gave her a worried look. "No condom. I'm clean though, I swear it." Before Mandy, he hadn't had sex for a long time. Too long to think about.

"Me too. And stop worrying, I've got us covered. I'm protected." She smiled wickedly. "I like it better without the condom."

He breathed a sigh of relief.

"I never knew it could be like this," she said, cupping his face. Her eyes shone with adoration. "Thank you."

Overcome with emotion he didn't know what to do with, he kissed her softly, picked her up, and carried her to the bedroom.

* * *

Amanda was surprised that Joe was still fully clothed. She'd lost herself to the sensations he created, forgetting her surroundings. Forgetting everything except his touch. His hands on her, his mouth marking her neck, his cock filling her. Never had a man taken the time to ensure her pleasure. And he didn't just ensure it. He got off on it. She'd felt the heat from his erection as it brushed her ass, the tension in his body as she moved against him. She'd broken his control. He'd fucked her like an animal and she couldn't have been happier.

She watched with womanly appreciation as he worked his way out of his clothes. She'd never get tired of looking at him. He had the kind of body that came from hard work and discipline. Not a spare ounce of skin. His eight-pack sported a thin line of dark hair that ran from his navel to his groin. It was the only hair on the wide expanse of his torso and sexy as sin.

"You keep looking at me like that, sweetheart, and I won't

be responsible for my actions." He slid into bed beside her.

She laughed softly. She luxuriated in the feel of his arms as they came around to pull her close. "You're so warm," she said as she burrowed into the crook of his arm, resting her head on his chest.

"Happy to be your blanket, sweetheart. Anytime."

She relaxed, content in his arms.

"So," he began, "tell me more about what you and your brothers do."

She drew in a deep breath as he caressed her back with his fingers. "We do a lot of things. Primarily private security training."

"Military training?" he asked when she didn't go on.

"We do a lot of private sector training, but yes, we also provide specialized training for the military." She gauged his reaction and saw nothing. No surprise, no calculating stare, no demand for more information. Just the quiet stare of a man relaxed in the arms of his lover.

She moved on. "Our bread-and-butter comes from our thousand-acre private training facility." Ah, that got his attention. "We train private as well as military personnel. We've got weapons ranges, compounds set with explosives, off-road driving tracks, the works." She laughed as his face lit up with a silly grin. She playfully swatted at him. "You're such a guy."

"And you?" He laughed. "What's your role in all that?"

"I don't get to spend much time on-site. Caleb and Brandon lead the teams, but we have a great group of guys to handle the day-to-day stuff. Alec fills in too, but I think he just goes out there so he can play on the off-road tracks. I'm in the office most days, working on private security jobs that come in."

"What kind of private security jobs?"

"Mainly helping people secure their own systems. Whether it's computer systems or electronic security systems. I find the holes and plug them. Sometimes it's not very challenging. It can be extremely tedious and boring even, but the pay is great." She gave him a coy smile. "I'm good with computers. Really good, actually. Me and Alec, we're what I guess you could call the hackers of the group. There isn't much we can't do with a computer"—she winked at him—"or a cell phone and some duct tape."

A comfortable silence fell over them. She liked that he didn't press her for more. He took what she gave him. Just another thing to add to her list of things she'd miss when she went home.

God, home. Her apartment in the city had never felt less like home than it did in this moment. She loved it here in this warm and cozy house, rustic and comfortable. Not the modern version of her life in the city. An immense wave of sadness overwhelmed her.

"Hey baby," Joe soothed as if knowing the direction of her thoughts. "I lose you somewhere?"

"Tell me more about you," she said quickly. "How did you end up owning the bar?"

"Not much to tell, really. I suppose you could say I was tired. Tired of living out of a pack. Tired of the constant moving around. I'd served my country well, and then I was done. It was time to see what I could make of the rest of my life." He shrugged. "I wanted peace. I needed quiet."

"So you, um, bought a bar?" she teased.

He barked out a laugh. "Seems crazy, doesn't it?" His voice grew serious. "What I needed most was a connection. I needed Jake. My flesh and blood. Something to remind me that I'm more than—"

"More than?" she prompted.

He cleared his throat roughly. "Our parents were gone. All we had was each other. So I came home. It wasn't easy. Jake wasn't as welcoming as I'd hoped. We fought a lot. He was making extremely poor choices, as kids his age do. He'd been on his own for a while and didn't want me bossing him around. I'd been on *my* own long enough to forget how to *do* the bossing." He chuckled. "There is a fine line between bossing and bullying. Walking that line takes a finesse I didn't have. I gave 'bull in a china shop' a whole new meaning.

"I was about at my breaking point when I stopped in at The Wild Pony to have a beer and clear my head. It was a slow afternoon, just a few people playing pool and me. The owner was tending bar and we got into a discussion about his business. He hinted at wanting to retire, so I offered to take the bar off his hands."

"Just like that?"

"In a nutshell, yes. I'd made a lot of money and never had any reason to spend it, other than sending some to Jake each month to cover his expenses. We reviewed the financials and I made him an offer he couldn't refuse. I looked at it as a way to put down roots. Something Jake and I could do together. I wanted to prove to him I wasn't going anywhere. I wanted to give him the stability he never seemed to have, even though he's lived here his whole life."

"What happened to your parents?" she asked gently.

"My mom died just after Jake was born. There were complications from his birth that she was never able to recover from. I was ten at the time. All of a sudden it was just me and my dad and this little baby neither of us really knew what to do with." He looked down at her. "Dad kind of checked out for a while, so the responsibility for Jake was on me. Then Dad just turned cold. I think losing my mother was too much for him. He couldn't deal with her loss so he just turned himself off, went through the motions of his life until it was over."

Amanda turned, placing her hands on his chest. She rested her chin on her hands and looked up at him. "It sounds like they were very much in love."

The crease in his brow deepened. "Maybe. I don't really remember. I have bits and pieces of memories of them together." He hesitated a second. "I remember them always laughing and touching, so maybe ... yeah. I guess they were."

"So you raised Jake? When you were ten?"

He shrugged a shoulder. "I guess you could say that. Dad was always there. He made sure there was food in the house. He did what he had to do if I wasn't there, but he sure never lifted a finger if I was." Resentment oozed from his voice. "I started to hate Jake for taking away the mother I loved and for ruining my life. I started staying away more and more. I stole one of my dad's pistols and a box of bullets and I started target practicing. I figured out pretty quick that if I was shooting, I could forget about everything. It helped me manage my anger, gave me something else to focus on."

"Practicing where?" she asked, incredulous. "How old were you?"

"Jake wasn't quite two yet, so I was about eleven or so. I shot not far from here, actually. In the woods just a few miles back. I had the whole thing set up. I used whatever I could find for a target. Empty cans, bottles, coffee cans, you name it. Once that lost its challenge, I took to hanging things from ropes in the trees. Moving targets presented a greater challenge so I'd go out on the windiest days. I earned a little money here and there to replenish the bullets, but it wasn't long before I got caught."

"Your dad?"

"Nope. Old Sheriff Jackson."

"I remember him." Amanda pictured the aging man who used to come by when her family was here. "He always brought me those little butterscotch candies."

"I'm not surprised. He always had a pocketful," Joe said with affection. "Turns out I was a crack shot by the time I was thirteen. Sheriff Jackson would let me use the police range after school. Then, he set up a new range just for me. Longer distances, moving targets, the works. He also started letting me shoot other weapons from his personal collection, which was pretty extensive. It gave me the opportunity to hone my skills, but in all honesty, it came naturally to me. Needless to say," he said without humor, "I was recruited very early."

"A sniper," she whispered more to herself than to him. Understanding dawned. "You came home to remember that you're more than a sniper, is that it?" His body went rigid and she rushed to reassure him. "Don't you see? You *are* more. So much more."

His chest deflated as the air left his lungs. "It's all I know, Mandy. It's all I've ever done." The sadness in his voice tore at her heart. "I don't want death to be my legacy."

She smoothed his frown lines. "You raised your brother when you were but a child yourself. Then you came back to make sure he was taken care of and so he wouldn't be alone. Whether you choose to see it or not, your legacy will be that of love." His arms tightened around her. "How did your dad take to you joining the military?"

He snorted. "He didn't say a word. He just looked at me. Then he got up and left the room. It was the last time I ever saw him." His eyes took on a faraway look. "He died a few years back. Heart attack. But if you ask me, he died the same day my mother did."

Amanda reached up and kissed him. "I'm sorry."

"You're just the sweetest thing, you know that?" He squeezed her tight. "There isn't anything to be sorry for. It took some time for Jake and me to get back on track, but we're good now. What about your folks?"

"Plane crash. I was fifteen. Since I'm the youngest, it sort of fell on my brothers to take care of me. Well, Brandon and

Alec anyway. Caleb had been gone for almost five years. I'm not gonna lie, I was horrible. I was angry at Brandon and Alec. When Caleb came home a year later I was angry at him too. I blamed him for everything."

"How did you get through it?"

"Sam." Her smile stretched from ear to ear. "She's the same age as Alec and was everything I wanted to be: daring and fun. She had no fear, no reservations. She started college early and was already on her own, which to a young girl like me was the coolest thing ever. She and Alec had been friends for a while so she used to come over to hang out with him. After our parents died she started hanging out with me a lot. She was this pretty girl with wild red hair who took pity on the plain-Jane girl who just lost her parents."

Joe looked surprised. "Plain-Jane? Darlin', do you not have a mirror? There's nothing plain about you." He smooched her nose.

She ignored him. "Sam and I became inseparable. We talked, we cried, we laughed. She let me be whoever I needed to be. She didn't judge. She was there for me, but she didn't hover. She let me grieve without fuss, unless I started feeling sorry for myself."

She laughed. "Then she'd rip my ass a new one.

"Caleb would tell you Sam's the troublemaker, but in all honesty it was just as much me as it was her." Joe looked skeptical. "Sam's a big talker. I think it's how she hides. I'm not saying she's a saint. Lord knows *that* would be a big pants-on-fire kind of lie. But she's not a bad person. Did you know her parents are rich?" She didn't wait for him to answer. "The kind of rich that most people only read about in magazines." His eyes widened with surprise. "Times twelve," she added dryly. "Sam doesn't talk about her family much. I get the feeling there are hard feelings there, but she won't talk about it." Concern for her friend bled through her words.

"The thing about Sam," Amanda continued, "is she has a heart of gold under all the gruff language and innuendoes. And if she cares about you, she'd give her own life for you. It's just who she is."

"So, tell me about the horsemen thing. What's that about?"

Amanda rolled over onto her back and burst into laughter. "I was sixteen. Caleb decided it would be good for us to come here, you know, to bury the ghosts of our parents, so to speak. We all loved it here and Caleb wanted us to be able to still enjoy it as a family, even without our parents. It was our first trip back after they died and we've rarely been back since." She shook her head. "Anyway, I was *not* looking forward to a week of testosterone overload, so I begged Caleb to let Sam come along. He flat-out refused. They didn't get along even back then. So I informed him of all the girly things he, Brandon, and Alec would have to do with me." Joe raised a brow at her, setting her off into another fit of laughter. "You know? Braiding hair, nail painting, shopping, makeup … that kind of thing."

"You're evil." He laughed.

"I know, isn't it great? But in the end, Caleb realized it was in the interest of their own sanity to let me have my way. About three days into the vacation, Sam and I decided it would be a great idea to raid the liquor cabinet and sneak off into the woods. I'm not sure how long we were out there. It had started to get dark and we were more than a little drunk. We were contemplating the pros and cons of starting a campfire while drunk when we heard this loud clumping noise headed right for us. We looked up to see these three horses bearing down on us with three very angry riders attached."

Joe burst out laughing. "Are you serious?"

"Completely." She giggled. "You should have seen them. I swear their eyes were flashing red. It looked like hell itself had opened up and dropped them out on top of us. Sam started waving her arms and yelling that the three horsemen of the apocalypse were coming for us. We started running. They chased us all the way back to the house. Thus the name was born." Amanda draped herself over Joe's chest and looked into his eyes. "I remember joking with her once, asking her what happened to the fourth horseman. I figured she'd say it was me, being their sister and all. But she didn't. She just laughed and said that one day I'd meet a man who'd fill the saddle." She gave him a sexy smile. "Congratulations. It seems Sam has given that honor to you."

She shrieked as he pulled her fully on top of him. "I'd rather fill you."

Her body came to life as she straddled him. She loved the feel of his calloused hands as they brushed across her nipples. She rubbed her fingertips lightly across his chest, delighting in the quiver that rolled over his skin. She teased the skin of his arms, trailing to his shoulders and up the sides of his neck. He growled and brought her down to his mouth. He didn't devour her as she'd expected. Instead, he pressed light kisses to her face. He kissed her forehead, the tip of her nose. He kissed her eyelids as he slowly entered her. "God, Mandy. I love how you're always ready for me. So wet and ready."

She tried to lodge him deeper, but he wasn't having any of that. He rolled until he was on top of her, his knees forcing her thighs wide. He returned to kissing her. His mouth trailed down the curve of her jaw. She felt the heat of his breath on her neck as he pushed farther inside her. She tightened on him, causing him to groan with pleasure.

His leisurely pace made her head spin. He worshipped her lips, her neck, her breasts. The stroke of his tongue matching the stroke of his cock. He filled her with excruciating precision. Slowly. Until finally, mercifully, he gave her every inch of him.

He entwined their fingers and brought their joined hands

above her head as he continued to rock into her. She wrapped her legs around him. She pressed her heels into his ass, trying to increase his speed. "Relax, sweetheart. There's no hurry." His voice was a husky rumble in her ear. "Let me love you."

She tightened her grip on his hands and gave herself over to him. He rode her slow and steady. Her arousal increased at the same slow pace. Her skin became sensitive to the slightest touch, making each caress an instrument of torture to her already aching need. The tenderness he showed her brought tears to her eyes. He blew a warm stream of breath over her collarbone, causing a delicious shiver to skate along her spine. When he took her mouth again, his gentle assault was her undoing. Her back arched as her whole body shattered. He swallowed her screams as his body continued to master hers.

She opened her eyes to look at him. She felt her breath leave her lungs with a loud *hiss*. His eyes shone with adoration. And there was something else. Something possessive. Something powerful.

Yes, yes, yes, her heart sang.

No, no, no, her mind screamed.

She quickly reminded herself, "It's just sex, it's just sex, it's just sex."

* * *

Joe stilled as he heard Amanda chant softly. *What the hell?* He'd been so consumed with her that he'd lost any semblance of time or space. There was only her. And yet…

It's just sex. His heart plummeted to his stomach as the words wormed their way into his brain. *It's just sex.* His body thrummed with the need to prove her wrong. *It's just sex.* A searing pain shot through his chest. Pain that was replaced by a cold realization.

She didn't want anything from him. She was still using him, even after the time they'd shared.

Jesus, he'd been wrong about her.

"Joe?"

Shit. She thought this was just about sex. For those first couple of days, sure. Well hell, maybe not even then. He wasn't sure it had ever been just sex for him.

Time to go. He eased off her.

She immediately reached out for him. "Wait, you didn't—"

"I need to go," he said abruptly as he jerked on his jeans.

"What? Wait a minute. I don't understand." Her eyes were frantic. "What just happened?" She reached for the sheet and drew it over herself, clutching it at her breasts.

"Nothing." He smiled at her. "It was great." He struggled to pull his boots on while standing up.

"It was great?" she mimicked. "What's wrong with you? You didn't even finish!"

"I finished you, didn't I?" His anger boiled to the surface.

She pressed herself against the headboard. "Joe?" Her voice sounded so small in the face of his anger.

He shoved his foot into a boot and stomped against the floor to finish the job. "Isn't that why I'm here, Amanda?" He bent his knee to adjust his pant leg. "You wanted a one-night stand and you got four nights. You should be more than satisfied." He spat the last word at her.

He knew he was being an ass, but he didn't care. The fact that she wouldn't face him pissed him off even more.

"Well?" he demanded.

Her eyes were shining with unshed tears when she looked at him.

"Oh no." He narrowed his eyes as he jabbed a finger at her. "No fucking way do you get to do that. No fucking way do you get to rock my world, say 'it's just sex', and then cry about it."

Amanda's eyes widened in horror as realization dawned. "Oh God. Joe. No ... I—"

"Save it," he snapped. He swiped his gym bag from the floor, tossing the strap over his shoulder. He hesitated in the doorway for a brief moment.

And then he was gone.

Chapter 9

Amanda sat rigid until she heard the front door slam. The sound of Joe's motorcycle revving up barely muted her distress as she burst into tears. There was no denying the hurt on his face. She'd done that, she thought miserably. She had caused the pain that burned in his eyes. And she wanted to take it back. More than anything, she wanted to see him smile and wrap his arms around her. God, she'd really messed things up.

Her body shook with the force of her sobs as she buried her face in her hands.

It was over.

She knew it would happen. It always did. But she never expected it would end like this. She'd been naive to think they'd kiss and hug, thank each other for a wonderful time, and then go their separate ways. The truth was much grittier when emotions were involved. There was no denying the emotion she'd seen in his eyes. The same emotion she'd felt reflected in her own.

She had fallen in love with him. The crushing weight of her

realization sucked the air from her lungs. She loved him and he was gone. Would it make a difference now if she told him? He'd left like he couldn't wait to be as far away from her as possible. She doubted he'd even talk to her.

She reached for his pillow and brought it to her nose. His pillow. Wrapping herself around it, she drew his lingering scent into her nose and cried.

The afternoon sun was blazing through her window when she finally rose, feeling more miserable than when Joe stormed out. She stumbled to the bathroom, squinting as the bright light burned her eyes. She stared at herself in the mirror. She looked like total shit. No real surprise there.

Dark circled her eyes, which had seemed to sink a little into her head. She ran her fingers gingerly over the vivid, purplish mark on the side of her neck. She could live without the zombie eyes, but that mark was one thing she wasn't in a hurry to be rid of. Joe's mark. She shivered as she remembered his frenzy to have her last night.

While she loathed the idea of washing his scent from her skin, she took the hottest shower she could stand. She washed and conditioned her hair, letting the force of the water beat away the tears that seemed to keep falling. She methodically went through the motions. She dried and dressed herself in her favorite jeans, a light T-shirt, and tennis shoes. She didn't even bother with her bra. Not as if she was having company or anything. She sat cross-legged in the bed while she worked a brush through her hair. The conditioner had done the trick so it wasn't long before she was tangle free. She felt detached as she gathered her wet hair into a ponytail, her mind already cataloging the things she needed to pack to take home.

Coffee. She needed coffee.

She desperately wanted to call him. In the end, she didn't. She was damaged goods. She didn't know how it happened or even when it happened. As she'd lain in her bed, alone and crying, she'd figured it out. She'd never completely given herself to a man before. She'd unknowingly held back, guarding her heart out of fear of being hurt.

The irony of the situation hit her dead in the face. The one man she willingly tried to hold back from ended up obtaining something no man ever had before. Her heart. And she didn't deserve him. Not after last night. He'd loved her so tenderly, so sweetly, and she'd ruined it.

She made her way downstairs to the kitchen. She was lost in thought as she poured the leftover coffee into the sink and refilled the carafe with fresh water.

As she turned back, a hand clamped down on her mouth; another came around her waist and held her tight. The carafe fell to the floor, the sound of glass breaking resonating throughout the kitchen. She tried to scream but the hand pressed down harder, digging painfully into her cheeks. She slammed her heel down on the foot she could see behind her as her fingers dug into any flesh they could find.

A definite male grunt sounded behind her. He released her just enough. She broke free and ran, hitting the porch before she realized she didn't have keys or cell phone. She didn't stop. Her feet tore up the distance between the house and the stable. She ran around the back and stopped, plastering her back against the side. *Who the hell was that?*

Her mind was racing almost as fast as her heart. Could Sam's stalker have figured out she was the one who'd helped relocate his wife? No. Sam had assured her there was no way to trace that back to her. Besides, she had a pretty good idea Caleb was keeping an eye on Vincent Matteo. If he was here, Caleb would know it.

What if he'd sent someone else? She risked a peek around the corner. Nothing.

She flattened back against the stable again as she quickly ran through her options. She couldn't risk running down the road where he was sure to catch her if he had a vehicle. Wait. A vehicle. She edged to the opposite corner and crouched down low. She peered around at the drive. Her car was there. She quickly scanned the area. No other vehicle in sight. *What the…?*

She glanced behind her at the woods. She could definitely hide there, but it wouldn't offer her much more than that. She couldn't run the risk of getting lost or turned around. *Dammit!* She needed to get to her cell. She'd left it charging in the office. She had to get back in the house.

As quietly as she could, she opened one of the stall doors just enough to squeeze through. She made her way to the area that would give her the best vantage point of the house. She risked a look out the window, but saw nothing out of the ordinary. Had her attacker given up and left? She sat down, drawing her knees up to her chest. She stayed silent, her mind frantically trying to grasp the situation.

Time stood still while she waited, listening hard for any signs of movement. Slowly gaining her feet, she glanced at the open area between her and the house. She breathed a sigh of relief. The coast was clear. She felt sure if whoever attacked her was still around, he would have come after her already. But she wasn't taking any chances. She'd get to the house, barricade herself in the office, and call the police.

Amanda carefully turned the latch and eased the door open. She filled her lungs with air and prepared to run. She didn't waste another second, bolting from the barn as fast as she could.

She'd made a wide path around her car when sudden pain shot through her scalp, hands grabbing her ponytail from behind. Amanda hit the ground hard enough to rattle her teeth. Before she could recover, she felt the sharp contact of knuckles against her temple.

Once. Twice. And then … nothing.

* * *

"Damn stubborn woman," Joe growled aloud to his empty office.

It's just sex. Who was she kidding?

He just had the most miserable night of his life, which had turned into an equally miserable day. He was furious. Over and over he'd played it out in his head. Every touch, every look, every word. Could he have misjudged her? No. He hadn't. She felt something for him; he knew she did. But she'd push him away because … what? Because they'd just met? It wasn't as though he was proposing to her. Although he rather liked the thought of her being his forever.

Her excuse of not being able to trust was wearing thin. There wasn't a doubt in his mind that she trusted him, cared about him. She was just too pigheaded to admit it. She'd convinced herself he'd leave even before she gave him the chance to prove otherwise. So what did he do? He'd left. Just like she'd expected. And it just pissed him the fuck off.

His cell phone went off for the third time. He dug it out of his pocket and looked at the caller ID. Caleb. Perfect. He was the last person Joe wanted to talk to at the moment. He tossed the phone on the desk and resumed pacing.

"You're gonna wear a hole in the floor, bro," Jake said from the doorway.

"Fuck off, Jacob. Unless you're looking for a fight, I'd turn around and go back to the bar."

"Like that's gonna scare me," Jake said as he moved farther into the office.

Joe pinched the bridge of his nose. "What do you want?"

Jake gave him a worried stare. "You okay?"

The concern in Jake's voice quelled Joe's anger, leaving him tired and defeated. "I don't know, Jake. Yes. No." He pulled at his hair before jamming his hands into the pockets of his jeans. "I feel like I've been split in two."

"No offense, bro, but you *look* like you've been split in two."

Joe started forward before he stopped himself. What was he going to do? Beat the shit out of his brother? Not helpful. So instead, "Get out, Jake."

"Do you love her?"

The unexpected question jolted him. He stared hard at his brother. "Yes."

"Then tell her," Jake said simply. "No games, no pussyfooting around. If you think you can spend your life with her, then for the love of God, don't let your stubbornness get in the way." He lowered his voice in warning. "Don't let *her* stubbornness get in the way either. If you love her, she's got a right to know. Regardless of the outcome."

Joe didn't know what to say. Jake was right. When did he get so smart?

Jake clapped him on the shoulder and turned to leave. "Oh, by the way," he said, tossing Joe the cordless bar phone. "Some guy named Caleb Martin. He said it's urgent."

Joe snatched the phone and glared at him until he retreated from the office. He brought the phone to his ear. "Look, Caleb, I—"

"Is Amanda with you?" Caleb's concern drifted through the phone line.

"No." He really didn't want to get into this with him right now.

"Well? Where the hell is she?"

Caleb's tone brought the hackles up on the back of Joe's neck. "I don't fucking know where the hell she is. I assume she's at the house where I left her. We sort of … we had a fight." Maybe he did want to get into it after all.

"What did you do to her?" Caleb demanded.

Joe took a deep breath and counted to ten. Then to twenty. "Well?"

Joe snarled into the phone. "I fell in love with her, you dumbass. That's what I did."

Silence.

Joe continued. "I love her." His voice was filled with conviction. "Can you believe she actually had the audacity to say it's just sex between us? We both know good and goddamn well it's more than that."

"Whoa. Easy on the sex talk there, Sterling. That's my sister you're talking about."

"You know what? Bite me. Your delicate sensitivities aren't my problem."

More silence. Joe was happy to ride it out. He didn't want to have this conversation, but even he realized Caleb could be a powerful ally when it came to Amanda.

"She's got issues, Joe," Caleb finally said quietly. "Abandonment issues, if you know what I mean."

Joe snorted. "Ya think?"

"It hasn't been easy for her," Caleb defended. "She was young when I joined the military. She was pretty angry when I left. She definitely got the Martin family temper. You should have seen her. This little ten-year-old sprite with blonde curls. I can still see the fury in her little face as she stood on her tiptoes and faced off with me. She accused me of deserting her. Deserting the family. It was like being chastised by a cherub." He chuckled before going on. "Jesus, Joe. I wasn't more than a kid myself. Barely seventeen. I knew Amanda looked up to me, but I never believed my leaving would cause her any harm. She was just my pesky little sister. I figured she wouldn't even miss me with the other two around to give her grief. I sent her letters and postcards and she still refused to talk to me. Girl has a stubborn streak a mile wide."

Joe imagined the little girl Caleb described. His Mandy. So full of fire, so full of passion, so full of love.

"Then our parents were killed." Caleb's voice brought Joe back to the conversation.

"What happened?" he asked, hoping Caleb could fill in the gaps for him.

"We don't know much. The private plane they were on went down over the Rockies. An unexpected storm blew in and, well, we can only speculate as to what happened. There were five other people on board, no survivors. Amanda changed after that. She closed herself off. Brandon and Alec tried to be there for her, but they were angry and grieving as well. No one knew what to do for her." Caleb went silent.

"And then you came home."

"Yes. My time was up anyway, so after our parents died I decided to get out. We were left with a hefty sum of cash and a lot of property. My dad had a knack for business and made his investments very wisely. I started Martin Tactical and Security as a way for us all to stay together, even if it was just during the workday. Protecting others was all I knew how to do. Seemed right to pass that knowledge on to others. I failed miserably where Amanda was concerned."

"Amanda is an amazing woman, Caleb. You didn't fail her."

"Didn't I?" Caleb laughed harshly. "It all started with me. I was the first to leave her. Then our parents. Then the tools she decided to date." Caleb sounded like a man who carried the weight of the world on his shoulders. "But none of that matters now. What matters is that you understand why she pushes people away. I assume that's what happened between the two of you?"

"Your relationship with her is good now, right?"

"Nice deflection, but yeah. It took time, but she came around. I think she may even understand why I left. It was a crazy time and…" Caleb cleared his throat. "Did you tell her you love her?"

Joe sank into his chair. "No."

"Why the hell not?" Caleb barked.

"Because I want to keep her!" Joe yelled. "I get the feeling that telling her I love her after four days is a surefire way to send her packing. I'm having a hard time dealing with it myself. For chrissake, who the fuck falls in love in four days?"

"My sister did. With you. If there's one thing I know, it's Amanda. I knew the minute I saw the two of you together that it wasn't just a fling." He blew out a breath. "Listen, Joe, I get that you had a fight, but Amanda didn't check in with me today and she isn't answering her cell."

"She probably doesn't want to talk to you."

"Probably. But I'd still feel better if you'd check on her."

Jake poked his head in the office. "Joe? You need to come out here." As he started to refuse, Jake added, "Right now."

The urgency in Jake's voice caused a swell of dread to settle in his gut. "I'll call you back, Caleb," he said, disconnecting the call as he made his way down the hall and through the doorway leading to the bar. "What the hell is going on?"

Jake motioned to the man hovering by the door. "You need to hear this."

"Ernie?" Joe recognized the man. He and his pal Clete had been regular drinkers and pains in his ass until he'd thrown them out the other night. Generally they were just loud and obnoxious. But after they'd harassed Amanda, that was it.

He glared at Jake. "He better not be asking if he can drink here again."

Jake shook his head. "Listen." Jake motioned Ernie over. "Go ahead. Tell him what you told me."

Joe crossed his arms and widened his feet into a menacing stance. "Well?" he demanded. "Spill it."

Ernie was visibly nervous. He danced from foot to foot, wringing his ball cap in his hands. "My buddy, Clete. You know, the one who was here with me the other night?"

"Yes, Ernie. I know Clete."

"He's not a bad guy. Really he isn't. He just drinks too much is all. Just like a lot of folks do." Ernie nodded, agreeing with himself.

"Is this what you brought me out here for? To listen to him spew ode to Clete?" Joe hissed at Jake.

Jake snapped, "Ernie, focus."

"Right. As I was tellin' Jake here, Clete got bad upset about that girl hittin' him the other night. Started talkin' 'bout how she needed to be taught a lesson and shit like that."

Joe felt his face go hot with rage. Ernie rushed on. "I tried to talk him out of it. Told him she wasn't worth the trouble." He stumbled back as Joe growled dangerously. "He's been drinkin' bad since then. Talkin' crazy talk. When I ain't seen him around today, I got to wonderin' 'bout that girl."

Joe snatched Ernie up by his collar and resisted the urge to choke the living shit out of him. "What the fuck are you talking about?" he snarled. "What about Amanda?"

"Clete followed y'all the other night. Told me y'all left together and went to that big log house of hers."

Joe felt the blood drain from his face. The bastard knew where she lived.

"That's why I come to you when I ain't seen him nowhere. Figured he might try to make good on those things he was sayin'." Ernie shuffled his feet. "Ah man, I ain't never hurt a woman. Wouldn't want to see one hurt neither, if I could help it. So here I am."

Joe released him and took a step back. She hadn't checked in. "Does Clete have any weapons?" At Ernie's blank stare he tried again, only much louder. "Does. Clete. Have. Any. Weapons?"

Ernie shook his head in confusion. "Couple a huntin' knives maybe."

Joe turned to Jake. "Use the caller ID. Call Caleb Martin back and tell him what's going on. Tell him I'll call him when I get to Amanda." He sprinted back to his office. His hand was shaking as he turned the dial on his safe. He reached in and felt the cool metal of his .357 SIG against his palm. Within seconds he was locked and loaded. He slid the weapon into the waistband of his jeans and pulled his shirt down over it. He snatched his leather jacket off the back of his chair, shoving his arms into it as he moved back toward the bar.

Stopping only to grab Ernie and throw him into a chair, Joe snarled through clenched teeth. The small spark of violence did little to quiet the bloodlust that rampaged through his veins. "He goes nowhere, Jake," he commanded. "Keep his ass here and call the cops. Send them to Amanda's."

"Got it," he heard Jake call after him. His motorcycle roared to life and he wasted no time getting on the road. Gravel and dust sprayed, a sign of his haste to get to Amanda.

He prayed he'd be in time.

* * *

Amanda's head swam while she struggled to grasp what was happening. She was on the floor. The entryway floor. How had she gotten here? Why did her head feel like it was five times its normal size? She'd been outside. *Oh shit.* He'd grabbed her. Realization came fast, clearing the fog that filled her mind, and she scurried backward. She screamed when hands wrapped around her ankles and pulled her across the floor. She kicked her legs hard, tried to twist around to her belly, clawing into the wood of the floor.

She was jerked to her back. Pain exploded through her body when her attacker straddled her, pinning her arms beneath her.

She bucked her hips, desperately trying to get away. "Ain't you a feisty one." At his familiar drunken drawl, she froze. Her hands twitched as she remembered the feel of this one's jaw under her fist. Clete.

"Remember me, darlin'?" He leaned in until she could feel his breath against her face. The smell of beer and rancid meat made her gag. She turned her head and choked back the bile that burned the back of her throat. His fingers dug into her jaw as he forced her head back to look at him. "Ya gonna tell me not to touch ya now, little girl?" He slapped her face hard.

Fire blazed in the skin of her cheek, taking her breath away. She blinked back the tears that threatened to fall. He pressed his weight on her, severely restricting her air supply. She twisted, trying to release her arms. "Get … off … me," she gritted out, renewing her struggles to be free.

Clete ignored her. "Ya see, at first, I was just gonna come here and rough ya up a little. Ya know, teach ya a lesson 'bout what happens when little girls mess around with guys like me. But knockin' ya out outside wasn't as satisfyin' as I hoped. So I drug ya back here for what I really wanted." He grabbed her chin and shook her head from side to side. "Took ya long enough to wake up." His gaze drifted to her chest. He licked his dry, cracked lips.

"I followed ya," he sneered. "That night. I watched ya 'bout fuck that guy outside. Watched ya wrap yer pretty little legs around him. Givin' him what I wanted." He tore the front of her shirt open, leaving her bare to his gaze. "So now I'm thinkin' ya owe me a little of what ya screamed for him."

Amanda didn't even try to follow his drunken logic. She shouted in fury as he palmed her bared breasts. She had to find a way out of this. Her gaze darted around the room, looking for a weapon. Something, anything to help her. Anything to distract her from the feel of his hands on her. "Scream all you want, darlin'. Ain't no one to hear ya." She gagged as he ran his tongue up her cheek. "I'm thinkin' to take my time with ya. Enjoy ya right good."

He was stinking drunk, thank God for that. Drunk men weren't rational.

Keep him off balance.

Amanda curled her lip. "You aren't gonna enjoy jack shit if I have anything to say about it." She braced herself for another hit. It came hard and fast. The tangy taste of blood hit her tongue as she felt her lip split open. She didn't even try to stop the tears that streamed down her face. "That all you got?" she said as she fought to shake her vision clear.

He growled at her. As his hand came around her throat, she caught a glimmer of silver from his belt.

A hunting knife.

"Shut up, bitch!"

She was frantic now. She needed him to come closer. She shuddered at the thought, but it was her one shot. Maybe her only shot. "Some man you are, you slimy bastard," she ground out.

He swayed above her, watching her with disbelief. "What's that?" He leaned down to get nose to nose with her, loosening his grip on her throat. Amanda gasped for air, using all of her strength to smash her head into his. She felt the bridge of his nose give way under the hard bone of her forehead. Just like her brothers had taught her.

He yelled out as he leaned back and clutched at his nose. He looked down in shock at the blood that flowed into his hands. She twisted violently beneath him and pulled her arms free.

She didn't ... wouldn't think. She grabbed for the hilt of the knife on his belt. The minute the knife cleared the sheath, she plunged it into his thigh. His scream filled her ears as she pushed away from him. She got to her feet and ran toward the kitchen.

Just as she cleared the doorway her feet were pulled out from under her again and she went down hard.

"I'll kill ya for that, bitch."

Amanda felt something warm run down her forehead. This was it. She'd taken her chance and lost. Dizziness overwhelmed her. She watched in wonder as a large shadow formed behind Clete. She imagined her knight in shining armor coming to save her. "Joe," she whispered before everything went black again.

* * *

Joe kicked through the front door just in time to see Amanda hit the ground. He cursed and grabbed Clete by the back of the neck. He watched with horror as blood ran down Amanda's forehead. His blood ran cold as he saw the skin exposed by her torn shirt, his gut clenching at the thought of another man's hands on her, hurting her. His body shook with the need to kill the motherfucker who'd touched her. The motherfucker he had in his grip.

Joe slammed Clete into the floor and grabbed the hilt of the knife still sticking out of his leg. "If anyone is gonna die here today, it's you, you fucking asshole." Clete cried out as Joe wiggled the hilt back and forth. "And I can make it take a long time."

"Joe?" Amanda's voice was weak.

Pushing Clete's face to the floor with a warning, Joe released him and rushed to Amanda. "I'm here, baby," he said, dropping to his knees beside her. He helped her sit up before pulling her into his arms. "Shh, it's going to be all right now. I've got you."

To his surprise, she pushed him away. "Get him out, Joe. Please, just get him out," she begged, her arms going around her legs a second before she dropped her head to her knees. "Just get him out," she repeated over and over.

Rage unlike he'd ever known blanketed him. He brushed

his hand over her hair before he stood. "You're safe now," he promised.

Rising to his full height, Joe moved like a predator, approaching Clete with deadly intent. He clamped his hand around Clete's throat and forced him to his feet. Joe tightened his grip, fully aware he'd stopped the flow of air. He pulled Clete toward the front door and outside onto the porch. He wanted Clete as far away from Amanda as possible. Joe tossed him from the porch, dust kicking up as Clete landed in the dirt with a grunt.

"Not so tough now, are you?" Joe stalked down the steps. He circled Clete, his anger all-consuming. His boot connected hard against Clete's rib cage before he moved around him once again. *More.*

Joe grabbed him by his shirt and yanked him up. The smell emanating from Clete made Joe's eyes water. "You wanna play, tough guy? How about you play with me, hmm? I guarantee it won't be like taking on a woman half your size." Joe slammed his fist into Clete's face. He grinned as Clete went down again, the sound of bones breaking under his fist filling him with satisfaction. "Ouch," he taunted, "that's gonna hurt when the alcohol wears off." *More.*

"Joe." Joe's head snapped around at the sound of Amanda's voice. "Enough," she pleaded.

Joe glanced back at Clete, anger still coursing through his veins. He clenched his teeth against the need to punch the fucker again. Clete watched him warily, his eyes dazed, although from pain or alcohol Joe wasn't sure.

Joe leaned over, his hands on his knees as he fought for control.

Amanda. His Mandy. Mine. Calm washed over him at the thought of her.

Clete moaned on the ground, his hands coming up

defensively when Joe knelt down beside him. "Consider yourself lucky, you piece of shit." For good measure, he reached out and pinched Clete's broken nose between his fingers. "If you so much as even think about Amanda again, I'll kill you."

"Joe, stop." He looked over his shoulder to see Amanda sink down on the top step of the porch, clutching the railing for support.

He released Clete and took a few steadying breaths before closing the distance between them. He stopped halfway, taking in the sight of her. She was the most beautiful woman he'd ever seen. She was here, alive and looking back at him with such emotion that he was swamped with shame over losing his shit with Clete. After all she'd obviously been through, she'd also had to snap him out of his rage. God, she was so much better than him.

He was a killer. He would've killed Clete and been more than happy about it.

She offered him a slight smile. Joe was in awe of the strength and resolve he saw in her eyes. He wouldn't disappoint her. No matter how hard he had to fight the urge to kill Clete—and he really wanted to kill him right now—he wouldn't do it. *She* was what mattered. Only her. He'd do whatever it took to be the man she needed.

Amanda looked past him and her eyes grew wide with alarm. "Behind you!" she yelled.

Joe spun back to Clete, who'd pulled the knife out of his leg and was gunning in his direction. He raised his forearm, feeling the sharp sting of the blade as it sliced through his skin. Twisting his arm over, he grabbed Clete's wrist and snapped it. The knife dropped to the ground with a thump, Clete following close behind.

Joe kicked the knife out of reach and snorted in disgust at the blood pouring from Clete's leg. "You stupid fuck. You'll probably bleed out right here." Joe ripped off his shirt and quickly tied it around Clete's leg, pulling it tight to slow the bleeding.

He grabbed his SIG and shoved the business end in Clete's face. "You move again and I'll add a bullet wound to your list of injuries. You get me?" Clete cradled his arm but said nothing. "Gotta put pressure on this wound," Joe said innocently as his boot came down on Clete's leg wound. He pressed hard, just to make sure he stayed put. Okay, maybe not just to make sure he stayed put. He may not be able to kill him, but he could sure make him suffer a little.

His brief glance back at Amanda filled him with a mixture of emotions. Seeing her wounds again renewed the rage that threatened to bubble over the surface. He felt like a volcano that was about to blow.

No, he couldn't look at her yet. Not while Clete was still within striking distance. He had a firm hold on the reins of his anger, but a man could only be pushed so far.

One thing he knew for sure. *She* wouldn't be pushing him away again. She was his. When this was over, she'd damn well know it.

* * *

It was total chaos. And perched on the porch steps, she had a bird's-eye view of the show. Swarming like locusts, police and medical personnel descended on her yard. Amanda watched with puzzled eyes at the three police cars parked in her drive, one belonging to the sheriff. Even though she couldn't remember exactly, she was pretty sure this constituted their entire force.

Joe had ditched his weapon, choosing instead to bind Clete's hands with rope he'd found in the barn while they'd waited for the police to arrive. He'd barely looked at her. In fact, he'd kept himself very busy with Clete, talking to her over his shoulder to ascertain whether she was okay or not. She was fine, she'd told him. All things considered, she rather thought that was the truth.

A tall, handsome man approached Joe. "What you got there?" she heard the man ask.

"Sheriff," Joe greeted, reaching out to shake his hand.

The sheriff shook his head slightly, gripping Joe's hand. "Since we've known each other all our lives, how about you cut the crap?"

Joe pulled him in and clapped him on the back. "Thanks for coming, Cooper. I'd appreciate it if you'd get this piece of shit off Amanda's property." He indicated an unconscious Clete.

Cooper whistled through his teeth. "Jake said Clete might have gone off the deep end. What happened here? He get mauled by a mountain lion or something?"

"Or something," Joe replied.

"You do all this damage?" Cooper asked suspiciously as he bent to check out Clete's injuries.

"Very little of it actually. He'd sustained the majority before I even got here."

"Well." Cooper stood and brushed off his hands. "He's still breathing."

Joe stiffened at Cooper's side. "He went after Amanda, Coop." His voice held a deadly edge. "He should thank his lucky stars he's still alive."

"Amanda?"

Joe nodded his head in the direction of her perch. "Amanda Martin. You may remember her; her family has owned this property for a long time."

"*That's* little Amanda Martin?" Coop said with interest. "I remember seeing her on occasion when I'd come out with my dad." He whistled. "As cute as she was then, I'm not surprised she grew up to be such a stunner."

Amanda tried to smile and gave them a quick wave to indicate she could hear them. She heard Joe mumble something under his breath as Cooper approached her.

"Amanda? I'm not sure if you remember me." Cooper approached her slowly, his hands clearly where she could see them. He eased down on the step below her, as if trying to stay as unthreatening as possible. "I'm Cooper Jackson. My dad was the sheriff when you were younger."

"You got a pocketful of candy like your dad?" Amanda asked.

Cooper laughed and patted his pockets. Finding what he sought, he offered her a yellow-colored gem. "Like father, like son, huh?"

She laughed, quickly followed by a moan as she brought her hand to her split lip.

Coop reached out and gently touched her leg. "How about you let my guys check you out?"

"Coop?" Joe snapped. "Stop mauling her and get the fuck over here."

With a sigh and a nod to Amanda, Coop started back toward Joe. "Is that how you talk to your sheriff? How about a little respect?"

Amanda couldn't make out Joe's reply.

Joe and Cooper, along with several other officers, surrounded Clete as paramedics went to work on him. The men spoke in hushed tones, but as backs stiffened and hands turned to fists, Amanda knew Joe was relating the story of what had gone on out here. There was an aura of authority surrounding Joe that was impossible to deny. He oozed confident male as he stepped aside and let the officers take control of Clete.

Amanda waved off several of the men who tried to approach her. She didn't want the police or the paramedics. She wanted Joe. Why wasn't he coming to check on her? Her heart broke at the thought that she may have lost him. He had to know she hadn't meant what she said. How could he believe she felt nothing for him after the time they'd spent together?

Because I'd led him to believe it, that's why.

He'd come back, though. That gave her hope. She shuddered at the thought of how differently this night could have turned out if he hadn't.

A pretty female paramedic approached Joe with a friendly smile. Too friendly. Jealousy burned Amanda's gut as the woman attempted to look at Joe's damaged knuckles and wounded arm. Did she have to keep touching him? To Amanda's amazement, Joe seemed unaffected by the woman's attentions. Irritated even. He turned to the woman and bent to look her in the eye. As he spoke, the woman's cheeks turned bright red. Then she turned and stalked back to the ambulance. He didn't flirt with her or allow her to care for him. He turned her away as if she was nothing more than an annoyance. Amanda knew she shouldn't be pleased, but honestly, she was tickled pink.

An eternity passed before the ambulance and police cars finally pulled away. She'd continued to deny treatment from the paramedics and had absolutely refused to be hauled off to the hospital. After answering questions and having to withstand a stern warning from Cooper about taking care of herself or he'd be back, she and Joe were finally alone.

Butterflies bombarded her stomach as Joe finally came to join her on the porch step. He eased down next to her, not touching, not looking. He draped his arms across his knees and stared out at the corral. Though she wanted to speak, no words came. What if he couldn't forgive her?

For the first time since they'd met, the silence felt tense, awkward.

"You're bleeding," he said, breaking the quiet that engulfed them. "You should've let the paramedics treat you." His eyes gave away nothing, his expression emotionless.

She didn't hide the longing in her voice. "I'd rather you did it, if that's all right."

He nodded, shoving his hands into his pockets as he stood. "Can you walk?"

"Of course I can walk," she said as she stood, suddenly irritated by his indifference.

He nodded again, stepping back to let her lead the way.

CHAPTER 10

"You wouldn't look at me," Amanda whispered as they entered the bedroom. She moved past him to sit on the edge of the bed. Her hands played nervously in her lap, silent tears spilling from her lids.

Joe went to his knees in front of her. "God, Mandy. Please don't cry, baby. It's killing me." Which only seemed to make her cry harder.

"I wouldn't blame you if you hated me."

He lifted her chin so he could look into her eyes. "I could never hate you." He pressed his lips to her forehead.

"Why wouldn't you look at me? Outside? You ignored me." Her gaze returned to her lap. "I've screwed this up, haven't I?"

He took a deep breath. "Sweetheart, look at me." When her teary eyes met his he bit back a curse. "I've killed a lot of men in my time, Amanda. Bad men. I'm not going to hide it, nor will I deny it. Not from you. I did what I was ordered to do." He wrapped his hands around hers before he continued.

"I've never, *ever* desired to take a life. It was my job. Plain and simple. But one more look at you, Mandy. One more glimpse of your blood … of your"—his lips flattened—"of your torn shirt. That would have been it. Do you understand what I'm saying?" His grip on her hands was one of desperation. "I would have killed that motherfucker. It took every ounce of self-control I had to walk away." He drew a steadying breath. "Once we were alone on the steps, I didn't know what to do, what to say. I've never been as afraid as I was today. The thought of you hurt, of…" He blinked rapidly. "I lost it."

Her tears wet his fingers as he caressed her face. "I know it's not rational, Mandy. I know we've barely known each other a week. It doesn't make any sense at all, but I love you. I love that you're soft and girly, but tough as nails when you're pissed. I love the way your eyes light up when I walk into a room. I love the way you come apart in my arms."

He joined her on the bed, wrapping his arms around her and pulling her close. "I'm not asking you for anything, but you need to know I want to be with you. Not just for now, either. Loving you is the most important thing I've ever done. *You* are what I've been looking for, baby." He felt her shoulders shake with her sobs. He tucked her head into his chest and rocked her. "Ah hell, sweetheart. I know you don't trust me and after I stormed out last night I don't blame you. Sometimes I just need to clear my head. But I won't ever go far, Mandy, and I'll *always* come back. I'm not trying to pressure you. I can be a very patient man, so I'll wait. Just know this—whatever you need, whenever, however you need it, I'll be there."

Her sobs were ripping his heart from his chest. He didn't know what to do, so he just held her as she cried. He whispered encouraging words, told her how much he loved her, stroked his hands up and down her back. Little by little her tears began to dry until all he could hear was an occasional sniffle.

Finally she pulled away from him. He watched, fascinated, as she rallied her strength. With a sharp nod she said, "All right. Enough of that. Time to clean up." He followed her as she moved to the bathroom.

"Let me help," he offered as she reached for a washcloth. She nodded again and eased herself up to sit on the counter. He was worried that she hadn't said much or, well, anything really. Not that he expected her to throw herself into his arms and beg him to never leave. Hoped, maybe. But not expected. Anything would be better than her silence.

He wiped tenderly at the line of dried blood that sectioned her forehead, having come from somewhere beyond her hairline. Her left cheek was red, as if she'd stayed outside too long in freezing temperatures. She flinched as he lightly palpated the area. "Tender?"

She shrugged. "A little."

There was a bruise forming along her left temple. Her bottom lip was split and slightly swollen. Each wound caused knots to form in his gut, but he kept his expression light. He reached into her mass of hair to find the source of the blood. A cut, not too deep, was just above her hairline. She hissed as he brought the warm, wet rag to her head. "It looks like the bleeding has stopped." When she still didn't respond he said, "You'll need to shower to get the blood out of your hair. This rag isn't going to do the trick."

His gaze fell to the white-knuckle grip she had on her shirt. *Sweet Jesus.*

"Amanda, did he—"

"Don't."

"Tell me." He had to know.

The fury in her eyes caused him to step back. "He tried," she spat. "He would have succeeded if I hadn't stabbed him in the leg. He grabbed me, but he didn't do any real damage." She ran her tongue across her split lip. "Except to my face, that is." She gave him a slight smile. "I'm afraid he didn't fare as well."

God, he loved this woman. He released the breath he hadn't realized he was holding and shook his head in wonder. "I'd say not. You managed to stab him and break his nose," he said proudly.

"I broke his nose first."

He wrapped his arms around her and pulled her in close. "That's my girl." He buried his face in her hair. Every nerve ending in his body vibrated with joy at the feel of her in his arms. To have her here made him feel like the luckiest man in the world.

* * *

He'd left her alone to shower, promising to be just outside the door if she needed him. The warm water soothed her sore muscles as much as it washed away the dirt and blood. She took her time, carefully washing her hair twice and adding extra conditioner so brushing wouldn't further abuse her scalp. Once she was as clean as she could possibly get, she hurriedly dried off, applied her favorite lotion, and wrapped herself in a large towel. She caught a glimpse of her reflection in the mirror. She'd definitely had better days, but there was nothing she could do about that now.

He loves me. She hadn't completely screwed up, but she had a lot to make up for. She knew the sex between them had been incredible, but now she could admit it was because of the connection they had with each other. The connection made the sex amazing, not the other way around. He needed to know she understood that now. She needed to show him that she was his, that she wanted to be his, in every way imaginable. She needed it more than she needed her next breath.

He came to his feet as she walked back into the bedroom.

"Everything okay?"

She smiled somewhat apologetically. "My head hurts a little, but I took something for it so I should be right as rain in no time."

He looked unsure. He reached to touch her, only to draw up short. "I need to take care of my arm. Why don't you lie down and rest a bit. I'll be quick."

The mention of his injury got her attention. "Oh God, you're hurt! Let me see," she demanded, ashamed for not noticing before.

He smoothed his fingers across her cheek. "I got it. Really, Mandy. See?" He rolled his sleeve back and showed her the cut. It ran the length of his forearm. It was deep and vicious-looking, but had already stopped bleeding. "I'm trained to handle this kind of wound. Besides, I've had worse."

"Yes, I suppose you have." Her fingers traced over the cut. "It will scar," she said absently, her body already responding to the simple touch.

"Maybe," he said, drawing the syllables out. He bent to eye level with her. "Mandy? You okay, baby?"

The concern in his eyes reminded her of that first night. He'd asked her if she was okay then too. How quickly things had changed in such a short time. *Things never seem to go as planned, do they?* She sighed. "Yes, I'm good."

Was she? No. She wouldn't be good until he understood how sorry she was. And that she loved him too.

He seemed hesitant to leave her. "It's fine." She smiled at him. "I'll be right here when you come out."

She jumped into action as he disappeared into the bathroom. Her towel fell to the floor as she dug through her clothes and pulled out her sexiest nightgown. She held it up by the thin, delicate straps. It shimmered like a beautiful emerald, a perfect complement for her eyes. She slipped it over her head. The silk felt sinful as it caressed down her body. The bodice was made completely of lace, cupping her breasts, yet concealing nothing. There would be no hiding her arousal as her nipples were on proud display. She quickly decided to forgo the matching thong. The idea of being open and bare for him thrilled her. She ran her fingers through her wet hair, loving the way it felt as the cold strands teased her exposed back. The scent of her vanilla shampoo mingled with her jasmine-scented lotion to create a deliciously exotic combination she hoped he liked.

She collected Sam's gift basket and carried it to the bed. She wanted to erase the pain of the last twenty-four hours and replace it with memories they would cherish. No more sadness, no more pain. Only love and the passion that seemed to overwhelm them. She wanted only the memory of his hands on her, his mouth tasting her, his cock buried deep inside her.

She sat in the center of the bed and began pulling items out of the basket, looking for one item in particular. Funny, she'd never even considered having anal sex before. The initial thought of it had revolted her. Now, however, she felt a strange pride in being able to offer him a physical part of herself that no other man ever had. In this, he'd own her virginity.

When she pulled the small black object from the basket, her stomach contracted so hard she gasped. Her juices overflowed the walls of her pussy, trickling back and tickling over her anus. He'd teased her, given her a taste of what it could feel like. Now she wanted it all.

If she had her way, this would be a night they'd remember forever.

* * *

Joe's heart stopped dead as he walked back into the bedroom. There, sitting in the middle of the bed wearing a provocative little nightgown, was the sexiest woman he'd ever laid eyes on.

He took a minute to just enjoy the sight of her. The woman he loved. He had never been more sure of anything in his life.

"What do you have there?" He jutted his chin toward her fidgeting hands.

She looked up at him, her smile filled with sensual anticipation, and held the object up for him to see. "So … how does this thing work?"

His traitorous dick went rock hard as he recognized the toy from Sam's gift basket. "Um, Mandy." What was she thinking? She'd been attacked. Beaten and almost raped. *She's in shock. She's got to be in shock.*

"I've been thinking," she began.

"No, Mandy." His voice was firm. "We aren't doing this."

She feigned confusion. "We aren't talking?"

"That's not what I mean and you know it," he said gently. He couldn't take his eyes off the anal plug in her hand.

"As I said, I've been thinking." She held a hand up to shush him before he could interrupt. "About you and me." Her eyes were glued to his. "It's never been a matter of trust with us."

His brow raised in question.

"I get it now," she continued. "I doubted that I could ever trust another man, but I trusted you from the very beginning. I trusted you when I brought you home that first night. I trusted that you wouldn't hurt me and I've trusted you every second since. To say any different would be a lie." Her voice lowered to barely a whisper. "I was scared. I *am* scared." Then stronger, "But I refuse to let fear stop me from getting what I want."

He approached her slowly. "What are you saying?"

"I'm saying I was wrong. It wasn't—isn't—just sex with us. I said that more to convince myself, even when I knew it wasn't true. I'm saying that I'm scared because, even though we haven't known each other very long, my heart already belongs to you." She moved to him as he sank onto the bed. She wrapped her arms around his shoulders and pressed into his back. "I think, in some way, it's always belonged to you. *I* belong to you. You're the man I've imagined building a life with. Strong, loving, honorable ... and drop-dead sexy." She kissed his bare shoulder. "I'm saying I love you. I love you so much I ache with it."

He brushed a kiss against her temple. "God, Mandy, I love you so much." He hadn't intended to go any further, but her intoxicating scent drew him in. Her head fell to the side as he trailed light kisses down the length of her neck, losing himself in her taste, her scent. He returned to her mouth. Taking care with her split lip, he placed a soft peck at the corner.

Her moan filled his ears and she twisted herself into his lap. She pressed her mouth to his, her tongue flicking eagerly at his lips.

"Easy, baby. Your lip, your head," he cautioned. "You're in no shape for anything but rest tonight."

"I don't want to rest," she informed him. "Yes, today pretty much sucked, but we made it through. A little banged-up maybe, but I'm not as fragile as I look." As he started to protest, she placed a finger on his lips. "I don't want to look back on this day and just remember the bad. Help me give us something good to remember." She dropped the toy into his hand. "I want to share this with you."

He gave her a stern look. "Why?"

Surprise flitted across her face. "Partially because it's something you desire. Partially because I want to give you a part of me no other man has had." He couldn't stop the possessive growl that rumbled through his chest. "But most of all, it's because when I think of you taking me like that, it makes me all wet and achy." Her cheeks flushed a bright red. "Would you like to see?"

Damn, this woman pushed him to the limits of his control.

* * *

Joe's lips slanted over hers as he shifted her to straddle him. She curled her arms around his neck as he teased her with his mouth.

He placed a hand at her lower back and pressed lightly between her breasts, arching her away from him. The tiny straps of her nightgown snapped under his fingers and the material slid from her breasts. He cupped her, teasing the peak with his thumb. She shuddered as his teeth grazed over a nipple.

"Show me how wet you are, Mandy. Let me see how ready you are for me," he said against her breast. His mouth surrounded her nipple, his tongue flicking the sensitive tip.

"You're killing me," she rasped as his fingers worked their way inside her wet folds. He spread her thighs open, his gaze darkening as he exposed her hidden bud, swollen with need.

"Your pussy is so hot, baby. My fingers feel like they're on fire."

Bolts of pleasure surged through her, making her body vibrate like a live wire. Her fingers dug into the flesh of his shoulders. He stroked his thumb over her aching clit and she exploded with a cry. Her vagina pulsed violently as she spilled her release on his fingers.

"So beautiful," he whispered reverently. "Did you know that your nipples get harder when you come?" He teased a tip with his tongue. "I'll never get tired of seeing you like this. All flushed and blissful. You're so addictive, Mandy. So goddamn addictive, I could never get enough."

Her head fell back as he picked her up and shifted her back to the bed. He stood and undressed quickly. A thrill shot through her as she saw how hard he was. For her.

"Turn over, on your hands and knees," he directed, his voice dripping with arousal. Heat pooled in her stomach and she rolled for him, discarding her ruined nightgown in the process. Her breath hitched as his finger followed the seam of her ass down through her wet slit. "You're giving me a precious gift." He caressed the twin globes. "And I don't just mean this." She groaned as his wet fingers trailed back to tease the puckered opening to her ass. "I hope you weren't attached to the idea of using that toy, Mandy, because the only thing going in your ass tonight is me," he whispered as he slipped his fingertip into the tight channel. She tensed at the intrusion, the shock almost too much to bear.

"Relax, baby." He leaned over her and placed his mouth to her ear. "Trust me."

She had no intention of fighting him.

He pulled his finger from her, the burning bite of pain setting off a maelstrom of sensations.

Cool drops of lubricant, melted by the heat of her skin, made a slow descent down the seam of her rear. White-hot electricity shot through her pussy as the cool gel caressed her tiny hole. "Joe…" She didn't know if she wanted him to stop or if she was begging him not to. She was a slave to the feelings that overwhelmed her.

He moved in behind her. "Your ass is so gorgeous. So ripe and ready for the taking." He eased a finger, slick with lube, back inside her. He took his time, easing in and out, preparing her for his ultimate possession.

She squirmed when he added another finger. Blinding pleasure mixed with the pain of his intrusion, driving her mad with the need to push him away and pull him deeper at the same time. He spread his fingers, stretching her, widening her. She hissed as liquid fire shot through her veins. Pleasure and pain became one. Her ass flexed as if by its own accord, drawing him in deeper.

"Are you ready for me, baby?"

She nodded as his cock replaced his fingers, pressing urgently against her entrance.

She couldn't speak. She dropped her shoulders to the bed as he pushed into her. She shook her head violently as the flared head slipped through her outer ring. *Oh God, he's too big.* There was no way she could do this.

He leaned over to caress her back. "Relax, Mandy. Let me in."

"I-I can't," she whispered.

"Do you want me to stop?" His cock twitched inside her. Heat burned through her anus as her pussy clenched with the need to come again.

"No, don't stop," she cried desperately.

He spread her cheeks wide as he began to move. His slow, shallow strokes brought a sheen of perspiration to her skin. She could feel every pulsing vein in his hard shaft as he worked himself inside her.

"You feel so good, so hot and tight around me, Mandy," he grunted as he surged into her, burying himself to the hilt.

"Oh, God." The pressure in her womb built to an agonizing level. She felt full as he stretched her to the limit. Her hands fisted in the sheets as he began to ride her. Each thrust in her ass caressed the walls of her vagina, driving her to the edge of paradise. The pleasure/pain was so intense she knew she'd lose her mind. She wanted to cry. She wanted to scream. She couldn't breathe. She was burning alive. "Joe…"

"I've got you, baby," he said as he reached around and pressed against her clit.

Her scream resonated through the bedroom. Sparks lit behind her eyelids as she exploded. She gripped him in her orgasm, milked him until she heard his loud shout come from somewhere above her. She was floating, flying over the edge of paradise, and she didn't care if she ever came down.

She was barely aware of Joe moving from her. His light chuckle brought a smile to her lips as she stayed where she was, ass high in the air, but she didn't care. It seemed like too much effort to even slide down on the bed.

She moaned as she felt a warm cloth against her skin. Her heart was full to bursting as Joe gently ministered to her. She finally collapsed to the bed, grateful for his heat as he settled down behind her.

"There are no words for that," she sighed as his arms came protectively around her.

"Forget what I said earlier, Mandy."

She turned in his arms. "What?"

"Forget what I said about being patient," he said. "I changed my mind. I'm not going to be patient at all. You're mine, and I'm not letting you get away."

Amanda snuggled deep into his chest and hugged him close. "That works for me."

He stroked her hair. "So, you're okay?"

"I'm more than okay," she whispered, struggling to stay awake. "I'm in heaven. I love you, Joe … so much."

He laughed softly. "Heaven is wherever you are, baby. And I love you." He placed a kiss on the top of her head. "Forever."

Epilogue

Three months later

"You're giving me Fawn Glade?" Amanda fell into the chair and stared around the table at her brothers. They each had goofy grins on their faces as they nodded at her. She twisted around to Joe, who was pulling a six-pack of beer out of the fridge. "They're giving me the ranch?" she asked him. He placed the bottles in the center of the table and everyone reached in at once. The sound of tops popping filled the kitchen. Bottle caps were snapped in the direction of the trash, only to zing in chaos around the kitchen.

Skin-slapping high fives blended with the sound of laughter as the men debated who'd had the best shot.

Amanda laughed with them. "I still don't get it. Why now?"

Brandon reached across and gathered her hands into his. "You've been living here anyway," he said, leaning in to press a kiss to the back of her hands. "But don't think this lets you off the hook. We aren't gonna let you quit working with us"—he winked at the others around the table—"but we all agreed you can continue to do your part from here."

"You all agreed, huh?" she said suspiciously as she looked around the table, settling her gaze on Joe. He offered her a lazy grin. She was bowled over. He was so at ease, so relaxed in the company of her family. He was sprawled across his chair, his arms stretched wide, one resting on the back of her chair, one on the back of Alec's. They'd accepted him without reservation. He was one of them. And she loved him.

"I've already rewired the house with the latest and greatest," Alec chimed in. "For security purposes we're installing your own private servers here. I'll be over next week for the setup." He gave her a cheesy grin. "Joe is handling house and perimeter security. By the time we get done, this place'll be like Fort Knox."

"Sounds dreamy," she said sarcastically. To herself she mumbled, "And completely unnecessary."

"And it's not a bad commute for Joe to get to the training facility," Brandon continued.

"Just an hour or so." Alec nodded his agreement.

"Wait … what?" Amanda turned and poked Joe hard in the chest. "Since when do you need to commute to the training facility? What about the bar?"

Joe grabbed her finger and brought it to his lips. "Jake can run the bar just fine, sweetheart." His lips caressed her fingertips. "I'm just helping out while Caleb is"—his tongue darted across the sensitive pads as he nipped her—"otherwise occupied."

"Jesus, get a room," Alec complained.

"Otherwise occupied?" She narrowed her eyes and snatched her finger from him. "Stop doing that," she teased, and his laughter tickled her. She'd never get tired of that happy sound.

"Vincent Matteo," Caleb said to Amanda. "He's growing more desperate to find his wife. Samantha's car has been broken into, her tires slashed. She's received threatening voice mails."

"She told you she's received threats?" Amanda was skeptical. That didn't seem like something Sam would share with anyone, especially Caleb.

"Of course not." He grinned arrogantly. "I tapped her phone."

"Holy shit, Cay." Amanda shook her head. "You better hope she never finds out."

"Like I give a shit if she does. She may not care that her life is in danger, but I'll be damned if I will just sit back and let her roll out the welcome wagon for this fuck-nut. He's desperate," he repeated. "He'll screw up. When he does, I'll be there."

Amanda jumped out of her chair and threw her arms around her brother. "Thank you for watching out for her, Cay. I love you." She gave him a big, sloppy kiss on his cheek.

"All right, all right, jeez." Caleb peeled Amanda from him and pushed her back into her chair. "There's no need for all that. And I love you too." He jerked on her hair hard enough to make her gasp.

"Are you sure about this?" she asked.

"About saving the life of your stubborn-ass friend? Yep."

She punched him in the arm. "No, I mean about Fawn Glade."

Caleb smiled wide, his dimples flashing, "I never do anything I'm not sure about, kitten. We discussed it and we all agreed. He looked at Joe with a wicked grin. "Call it … well, call it a wedding present."

"A wed—" Amanda broke off as her eyes lit on Joe. "Huh?"

"Thanks a lot, dumbass," Joe grumbled to a still-grinning Caleb.

"What is he talking about?" Amanda demanded.

Joe pulled her chair around and took both her hands in his. "Obviously, I hadn't planned to do this now." He glared at the three pairs of watchful eyes. He gracefully slid off his chair onto one knee in front of her. "Amanda," he said, "will you marry me?"

"Wait, that's it?" Caleb complained.

"Dude, that was so lame," Alec added.

Brandon snorted in agreement.

"She knows all the mushy stuff." Joe's eyes never left hers. "Because I tell her every day, every chance I get, that I think she's the most amazing woman I've ever known. She knows that she makes me a better person. And she knows that I'll do everything and anything to make sure she's cherished, protected, and loved for the rest of her life." He raised a brow at her. "Right, Mandy?"

"Yes," she said softly, tears glittering in her eyes. "I know all that. And I know I'd love nothing more than to make you mine. Permanently."

He swooped in and captured her lips in a dizzying kiss. "I love you, Mandy," he whispered as the loud boom of a diesel truck came from outside.

A round of *what-the-hell* broke the mood.

Joe wore a shit-eating grin. "Perfect timing," he said as he pulled Amanda to her feet. "Come on, baby. I've got something for you." He pulled her behind him and out to the porch.

At first, she didn't understand what she was seeing. A truck pulled through, carting a large horse trailer. The driver maneuvered until the trailer door was backed up to the gate of the corral.

"What's all this?" she asked.

"Look." Joe jutted his chin toward the action.

"Oh my God!" She squealed with delight as she watched the magnificent horses descend into the paddock. Four of the most beautiful black stallions she'd ever laid eyes on. "They're gorgeous," she gushed.

"In honor of you and Samantha," Joe said and bowed

regally to her.

"Four horses for the four horsemen!" Amanda clapped her hands and dissolved into a fit of giggles.

"You've got to be fucking kidding me, Sterling. You don't have to encourage them," Caleb said with disgust.

"On the contrary. I plan to encourage them for the rest of my life."

Brandon and Alec jogged off to meet the new additions. Amanda threw her arms around Joe and squeezed him tight. "I love them!" She peppered his face with kisses. "Are you going to take me for a ride?"

Joe's grin about split his face. "Oh baby, I'm gonna give you the ride of your life, believe me."

"Oh, for fuck's sake." Caleb shook his head as he turned to follow his brothers.

"I love you, Joe." Her heart was filled with happiness as she looked at him. "You're the best one-night stand ever."

He returned her smile. "That was the best night of my life, Mandy, because now you're mine forever."

She jumped up and wrapped her legs around his waist. "Yes, mine forever." She kissed the tip of his nose. "Now, about that ride…"

The Martin Family story continues in SHADOW OF SIN. Available now!

Here's a preview of what's in store as Caleb Martin faces his worst fear. His past.

PROLOGUE

Columbia

2001

He was going to die out here.

The smoke set his lungs on fire, forcing him to take shallow breaths. It hurt like hell to take a deep breath, pushed him too close to the edge he already teetered on. His eyes watered, the pain in his leg and shoulder damned near unbearable. He fought against the pain. Mind over matter. He was a Marine. He could do this. He had to do this.

Had to stay conscious and, preferably, alive.

Quiet. So fucking quiet.

He was on the ground, knew that much by the blue sky above him, beyond the haze and trees that covered the remote location.

They hadn't been equipped for a fight like this. Not here. Not now. It should've been a cakewalk. Get in, get out.

Not a fucking bloodbath.

His men. Son of a bitch. He arched his neck, looking for his downed team, and immediately regretted the movement. He clutched a fist against his wounded shoulder and panted for air. Where were his men? For that matter, where was he?

They'd gone down. Every one of them. Shaw. Riley. Morgan. Stephens. As if in slow motion, one-by-one they'd fallen as he took rounds meant to kill him—and likely still would.

They'd been ambushed. Surrounded with nowhere to go, no time to gain cover. And then … shit. He reached for the sheathe strapped to his leg. Empty. He'd drawn his knife and buried it into the belly of … the man who'd dragged him away. To the safety of the jungle.

What. The. Fuck?

He shook his head, struggling to clear the fog from his brain. This was cartel territory. Their intel had provided an opportunity to quickly and quietly take out one of the top men in this area, thereby crippling the shipment of drugs to the United States, at least temporarily. Intel that had been wrong, if the number of men, armed to the teeth, who'd overtaken them was any indication.

Too many questions. Who was the man who'd dragged him out here, away from the site? Where was he now? Why the hell hadn't he left him a weapon?

And why was it so goddamned quiet?

Groaning, he slowly pushed himself up. The world swayed, seducing him with the promise of unconsciousness. No, not yet. Not until he found his team. He was their commander. He had to find them. Owed them that much. It was his duty.

Dead was the only way he'd leave this jungle without them.

His injuries were severe. The bullet lodged in his right shoulder prevented any significant movement in that arm and hand. Blood seeped from his left thigh, saturating his pants. He couldn't see the damage, but he knew the bullet in his leg would kill him if he didn't do something quick.

He struggled to unlatch his belt and pull it free of his fatigues. His vision blurred as he wrapped it around his leg, above the wound, and fed the end back through the clasp. Taking two quick breaths, he pulled the belt tight and yelled out, his voice hoarse with the pain that exploded through his body. His hands shook as he secured the makeshift tourniquet and fell back to the ground, sweating, panting, praying he wouldn't pass out. Hopefully, it would slow the bleeding, buying him time to … he chuckled. To what? He was in the middle of the jungle. Wounded and unarmed. He was a sitting-fucking-duck.

This was supposed to be his last mission. He was going home to his family. A family left shattered in the wreckage of the plane crash that had killed their parents last year. Now, it seemed he'd only add to the wreckage by going home in a box.

His men were dead. Fathers, sons, brothers. Men under his command, his protection. Gone.

His father had hounded him on the importance of family. Of living by his word and doing what was right. As the oldest son, it was his responsibility to live by a certain set of rules.

Family. Honor. Duty.

Concepts his seventeen-year-old self hadn't accepted from the father who'd loved him. He'd left home then, joined the military. It was there he'd finally understood what his father had tried to teach him. It was there he'd dedicated his life to protecting others.

And he'd failed. The fact that his men were dead and he was laying in a puddle of his own blood was evidence enough.

What would happen to his family now?

There were so many things he wished he'd said. Regret was a nasty bitch.

He watched the trees sway, concentrating on the back and forth motion as he battled with his body for the upper hand. He wasn't ready to go. Seemed his body had other ideas.

His eyelids grew heavy. So tired. Maybe he should rest a bit. Regain his energy so he could get them out of here. Somehow.

Brandon. Alec. Amanda.

Chilling cold raced through his veins as the feeling left his limbs.

He'd failed them all.

If, by some miracle, he survived … never again. Whatever it took, he swore to himself then and there.

I'll not fail them again.

But first, he needed to rest. Just for a minute. His strength depleted, unable to fight any longer, Caleb Martin embraced the darkness.

Oblivion the only salvation from his sins.

ALSO BY PARKER KINCADE

THE MARTIN FAMILY SERIES:
One Night Stand
Shadow of Sin

ANTHOLOGIES:
Lucky's Charms
Love in the Cards

GAME ON SERIES:
Spring Training

SHADOW MAVERICK RANCH SERIES:
White Collar Cowboy
Borrowed Cowboy
Cowboy Redeemed
White Collar Wedding

STAND ALONE:
Devlin

ABOUT THE AUTHOR

National Bestselling Author, Parker Kincade, writes edge-of-your-seat-sexy romantic suspense, hot and steamy sports romance, and erotic western romance. Her first novel, One Night Stand, won the 2013 Reader's Crown Award for Best First Book, the category of Best Erotic Romance in the Celtic Hearts Romance Writers Golden Claddagh contest, and was named finalist in the Romance Writers of America/Passionate Ink Stroke of Midnight contest.

Parker lives in the southern United States. She loves to read, play golf, spend time with her family and friends, snuggle with her beloved boxer, ice cream from the ice cream truck, and watching old musicals.

SIGN UP FOR PARKER'S NEWSLETTER!

To receive all the latest news and appearance information for Parker Kincade, please join at http://www.parkerkincade.com/Newsletter.htm

Find Parker Kincade Online:

Website: www.parkerkincade.com
Blog: www.parkerkincade.blogspot.com
Facebook: www.facebook.com/parkerkincade
Twitter: www.twitter.com/parkerkincade
Goodreads: https://www.goodreads.com/author/show/6475101.Parker_Kincade

Made in the USA
Las Vegas, NV
01 September 2022

54530975R00095